Summer 1999 Vol. XIX, no. 2
ISSN: 0276-0045 ISBN: 1-56478-221-2

THE REVIEW OF CONTEMPORARY

T0166632

Editor

JOHN O'BRIEN
Illinois State University

Senior Editor

ROBERT L. MCLAUGHLIN
Illinois State University

Associate Editors

BROOKE HORVATH, IRVING MALIN, DAVID FOSTER WALLACE

Book Review Editor

AMY HAVEL

Production & Design

TODD MICHAEL BUSHMAN

Editorial Assistants

BRIAN BUDZYNSKI, JOSHUA GULICK, LORI LITTLE, KRISTINE PRIDDY,
MEGAN WHITE, KRISTA VEZAIN

Cover Art

MARCEL DUCHAMP (American, born France, 1887-1968),
*The Bride Stripped Bare by Her Bachelors, Even (The
Large Glass)* c. 1915; Philadelphia Museum of Art:
Bequest of Katherine S. Dreier

visit our website: www.dalkeyarchive.com

The Review of Contemporary Fiction is published three times a year (January, June, September) by The Review of Contemporary Fiction, Inc., a nonprofit organization located at ISU Campus Box 4241, Normal, IL 61790-4241. ISSN 0276-0045. Subscription prices are as follows:

Single volume (three issues):
Individuals: $17.00; foreign, add $3.50;
Institutions: $26.00; foreign, add $3.50.

DISTRIBUTION. Bookstores should send orders to:

Dalkey Archive Press, ISU Campus Box 4241, Normal, IL 61790-4241. Phone 309-438-7555; fax 309-438-7422.

This issue is partially supported by a grant from the Illinois Arts Council, a state agency.

Indexed in *American Humanities Index, International Bibliography of Periodical Literature, International Bibliography of Book Reviews, MLA Bibliography,* and *Book Review Index.* Abstracted in *Abstracts of English Studies.*

The Review of Contemporary Fiction is also available in 16mm microfilm, 35mm microfilm, and 105mm microfiche from University Microfilms International, 300 North Zeeb Road, Ann Arbor, MI 48106-1346.

visit our website: www.dalkeyarchive.com

THE REVIEW OF CONTEMPORARY FICTION

BACK ISSUES AVAILABLE

Back issues are still available for the following numbers of the *Review of Contemporary Fiction* ($8 each unless otherwise noted):

DOUGLAS WOOLF / WALLACE MARKFIELD

WILLIAM EASTLAKE / AIDAN HIGGINS

ALEXANDER THEROUX / PAUL WEST

CAMILO JOSÉ CELA

CLAUDE SIMON ($15)

CHANDLER BROSSARD

SAMUEL BECKETT

CLAUDE OLLIER / CARLOS FUENTES

JOHN BARTH / DAVID MARKSON

DONALD BARTHELME / TOBY OLSON

PAUL BOWLES / COLEMAN DOWELL

BRIGID BROPHY / ROBERT CREELEY / OSMAN LINS

WILLIAM T. VOLLMANN / SUSAN DAITCH / DAVID FOSTER WALLACE

WILLIAM H. GASS / MANUEL PUIG

ROBERT WALSER

JOSÉ DONOSO / JEROME CHARYN

GEORGES PEREC / FELIPE ALFAU

JOSEPH MCELROY

DJUNA BARNES

ANGELA CARTER / TADEUSZ KONWICKI

STANLEY ELKIN / ALASDAIR GRAY

EDMUND WHITE / SAMUEL R. DELANY

MARIO VARGAS LLOSA / JOSEF SKVORECKY

WILSON HARRIS / ALAN BURNS

RAYMOND QUENEAU / CAROLE MASO

RICHARD POWERS / RIKKI DUCORNET

EDWARD SANDERS

NOVELIST AS CRITIC: Essays by Garrett, Barth, Sorrentino, Wallace, Ollier, Brooke-Rose, Creeley, Mathews, Kelly, Abbott, West, McCourt, McGonigle, and McCarthy

NEW FINNISH FICTION: Fiction by Eskelinen, Jäntti, Kontio, Krohn, Paltto, Sairanen, Selo, Siekkinen, Sund, Valkeapää

NEW ITALIAN FICTION: Interviews and fiction by Malerba, Tabucchi, Zanotto, Ferrucci, Busi, Corti, Rasy, Cherchi, Balduino, Ceresa, Capriolo, Carrera, Valesio, and Gramigna

GROVE PRESS NUMBER: Contributions by Allen, Beckett, Corso, Ferlinghetti, Jordan, McClure, Rechy, Rosset, Selby, Sorrentino, and others

NEW DANISH FICTION: Fiction by Brøgger, Høeg, Andersen, Grøndahl, Holst, Jensen, Thorup, Michael, Sibast, Ryum, Lynggaard, Grønfeldt, Willumsen, and Holm

THE FUTURE OF FICTION: Essays by Birkerts, Caponegro, Franzen, Galloway, Maso, Morrow, Vollmann, White, and others

Individuals receive a 10% discount on orders of one issue and a 20% discount on orders of two or more issues. To place an order, use the form on the last page of this issue.

Note from the Publisher

For those of you familiar with the *Review of Contemporary Fiction,* the present issue may seem to be at odds with what usually appears in these pages. So, a bit of explanation is in order. Philip Terry, who teaches at the University of Plymouth in Exmouth, England, submitted his novel to Dalkey Archive Press a few years ago, just at the time that the Press was cutting back on original works of fiction and reemphasizing its original mission of restoring to print major works of fiction that commercial publishers had allowed to go out of print. Under other conditions, we would have published Mr. Terry's work under the Dalkey Archive imprint.

I suggested to the author at the time that we might run his novel as a special issue of the *Review,* however, because it was so directly related to our ongoing interest in Oulipean writing, and asked if he would consider this option, as well as consider writing a critical piece describing his methods and perhaps asking David Bellos, Georges Perec's translator, to write on the novel. Mr. Terry agreed.

I believe that the quality of the novel speaks for itself; at another time in the United States, it no doubt would have been published by a New York house. But its appearance in the *Review* is due to, aside from its quality, the critical thinking provided by Mr. Bellos and the author, providing us with a glimpse at the Oulipean methods employed and a very good critic's commentary on the results.

David Bellos is the primary translator of the works of Georges Perec, including *Life: A User's Manual* and *W or The Memory of Childhood,* as well as the author of Perec's biography, *A Life in Words.* He teaches at Princeton University.

JOHN O'BRIEN

contents

Introduction
The Book of Bachelors *by Philip Terry*

These somber and often funny tales of bachelor lives—very British lives, I might add, ranging from that of a Tesco store detective to a monkish verger, from that of a dustman to a secondhand bookseller's assistant—are at the same time exactly what they seem and something quite else. Philip Terry's stylish evocations of solitary desire from so many marginal positions in life (mental hospital, police surveillance, trash collection) are powered, or generated, by the very margins of writing itself.

All writers use rules of some kind—even the worst of Jeffrey Archers (and can there be worse than he?) follows rules laid down by tradition, by genre, by language, and by the imagination of public demand. Philip Terry has imposed upon himself a set of rules that do in fact come from a long tradition, even if they seem at first glance to be quite arbitrary. Most rules that we know were invented by printers or by their successors in copyediting offices: to not split infinitives, to spell out numbers up to 99 in words, not to end sentences with "etc." and so on. But there can hardly be any form of verbal art that does not profit from constrictions of an altogether more signifying sort—be they utterly obvious to the eye and ear, such as the rhyming couplet, or perfectly hidden in the very substance of the text.

Among the boulevard entertainments of Restoration France, in the 1820s and 1830s, was a famous act, performed by many raconteurs but probably invented by a single genius. It involved telling a story five times over: in the first telling, no words with the letter *A* were used; in the second, no word with *E;* in the third, no word with *I;* and so on. Was it art? Hard to say. But the device, called a lipogram (or rather, here, a fivefold sequence of vocalic lipograms) harked back to the practices of the grands rhétoriquers of the sixteenth century, and even further back, to games played by the Romans and the Greeks. For there has been no period, not even the great era of laxity and *laisser-aller* that we call romanticism, when the need to find forms, constrictions, and rules of control has been entirely absent from the minds of poets and creators.

The *Ouvroir de littérature potentielle* (Workshop for Potential Literature, OuLiPo for short) was founded in 1960 by Raymond Queneau and François le Lionnais, with the specific aim of exploring the benefits that mathematics, and more generally, formal languages and explicit rules of conduct, could bring to the writing of literary texts. An almost secret group to begin with, a group with very modest ambitions for itself but vast ambitions for its intellectual and cultural project, it has become widely known and enormously influential in the course of its four decades of existence. It has already lasted far longer as a structured group than any other in the history of French (or indeed, European) literature: romanticism, realism, naturalism, Parnassianism, symbolism, acmeism, futurism, vorticism, surrealism, structuralism, telquellism—all such "doctrines" and chapels rose and fell within the span of a decade or two, and often far less. OuLiPo is very different and probably more important.

Queneau, born 1903, was drawn into the surrealist movement as a young man, and shared its interest in the unconscious and in dreams (he not only underwent psychoanalysis but gave an account of the experience in a fixed-form narrative). But he formed early on a view that remained stable throughout his long career, that art was not a matter of revolution nor a matter of untrammelled self-expression, but a matter of control. For complete freedom—most notably, in the almost parodic freedom of the surrealists' "automatic writing"—leads only to repetition. Queneau saw perhaps before most others that all surrealist poems resemble each other, just as all romantic novels tell the same story. Tools—in the form of rules—are required to allow the expression of the truly individual self.

Queneau disliked the idea of the poet as seer, prophet, magus, or genius. He saw no reason why verbal art should be any different from marquetry, painting, plumbing, or weaving—that is to say, a craft in the first place, then an art built on the basis of craft. This put him in a lonely position in the 1930s, the 1940s, even the 1950s, for no one among the reigning masters, be they surrealists (Breton), social realists (Nizan), moral humanists (Camus), or reactionary or revolutionary populists (Céline, for example), gave any place to craft in their pronouncements about the actual or necessary nature of writing.

OuLiPo is Queneau's revenge for the long neglect of his own work, which, even now, though enjoyed by many, is counted as marginal by most conventional histories of poetry and fiction in the twentieth century. In fact, the OuLiPo project arose almost as a consolation prize, as a by-product of a gathering held at the château of Cerisy-la-salle to honour Queneau's provocative campaign to revitalise written French by making it closer to the language actually spoken in contemporary France, a gathering that was itself the kind of consecration that marks the end, rather than the beginning, of a long career. Queneau was approaching normal retirement age, after all. And he knew that *Zazie dans le métro*, the only work that had reached a mass audience, was not the sole monument that he should leave.

The underlying project of OuLiPo could be summed up thus: given that people will go on using language to express opinions, to bare their supposedly inner selves, to influence others, and to pass on information, what else can be done with it? And by what means? The original members—mathematicians and computer scientists (Claude Berge, Paul Braffort), pataphysicians and renegade surrealists (Luc Etienne, Noel Arnaud), literary scholars and translators (Ross Chambers, Albert-Marie Schmidt, Stanley Chapman), the unclassifiable Marcel Duchamp, and the cofounder, François le Lionnais, a chess master, prestidigitator, polymath, and senior scientific civil servant—brought a huge range of skills and knowledge to the basic question and divided their work into two broad categories: first, to find out what else had been done with language in past eras; second, to borrow ideas and approaches from other disciplines of a formal kind so as to propose new ways of working with words.

It was not obvious that the project would achieve anything more than a bit of fun and few elaborate party games; minutes of the early meetings show that many members frequently feared that they may have been simply wasting time. It is true that some of the "rules" that were discovered or invented have remarkably little potential for creation: the most extreme example is perhaps the phonetic palindrome, a text which when read aloud and recorded on tape sounds exactly the same when the tape is played back in reverse. (Only one sentence in French corresponding to this rule has yet been found.) Others are so mind-bogglingly successful that the example-text seems to exhaust all the possibilities of the "rule." Queneau's own *One Thousand Billion Sonnets* is a case in point: just ten regular sonnets with the same rhyme scheme, printed in such a way as to allow each *line* to be turned over separately, generate ten to the power fourteen regular sonnets, more than Queneau could possibly have read in four lifetimes, let alone written in one.

But the group maintained its informal and cooperative atmosphere, meeting once a month for a meal and a worksession and imposing no rules of external conduct on its members at all. Unlike surrealism, OuLiPo was a liberal association of free men (yes, all men, until quite recently); Oulipians are not obliged to write with Oulipian rules; Oulipian rules are freely available to anyone who wants to use them. So the next stage of Queneau's project was to rejuvenate and to extend the group so as to include more writers likely to be energised by the experimental and partly iconoclastic aims of the group. It was by extraordinarily good fortune that the first new members to come along were Jacques Roubaud and Georges Perec, without whom, no doubt, OuLiPo would be less well-known in the world than it is today.

Perec in particular lapped up the knowledge in the OuLiPo's already substantial archive of forgotten devices and constraints. Because he was not gifted at mathematics himself, he focused at first most especially on rules that regulated the basic materials of writing—words and letters—rather than on the kind of complex combinatorial structures that only Berge and Braffort could really explain (the sestina, the bi-picture, and so on). And it was the very simplest of these rules, and one of the most ancient, that got him over his temporary writer's block.

Queneau himself had come across a curious American novel, *Gadsby*, by a California publisher, Ernest Vincent Wright, a novel written without the letter E. It is not a very interesting book, in fact; but the device of the lipogram, applied to the most frequently occurring letter in the alphabet (in English as in French) fired the group's imagination. What could be simpler? And what could be harder? And what would the successful implementation of such a rule prove?

It is now thirty years since Perec published *La Disparition*, and what seemed then like a completely insane, indeed almost unhealthy party game, can now be seen as a work of fundamental importance, not just for Perec, certainly not just for OuLiPo, but for the very possibility of verbal art. Philip Terry has not rewritten *La Disparition*: indeed, it is quite impossible to do so. But his *Book of Bachelors* shows that a real Oulipian constraint, once properly understood and implemented, allows a writer to create something truly individual and unique.

Why is this so? On first encounter with a rule as hard and simple as a lipogram, many people think that it will limit their expression and force them to say things they do not mean. But that would only be true if the rule is treated as an external constraint, as a layer of "translation" of some pre-existing expressive intention. A real lipogram—indeed, any real Oulipian exercise—is written from *inside* the constraint: that is to say, in this case, from inside the universe of meanings that are available in the vocabulary and syntax of twenty-five-letter English. And the striking result—verified in a thousand writing classes, in a thousand *ateliers d'écriture*—is that a text written under this sort of constraint is instantly recognizable as the product of this, not of that, individual. When we enter into a verbal world that is not natural, but limited by a material rule (that is to say, a rule that has nothing to do with meanings), then the things we find to say within it are somehow marked by our individual selves.

Perec did not discover this truth (all poets working in strict from have known it since the dawn of time), but he demonstrated it in a magnificent, flamboyant, and moving way; and his example has prompted many others, working in a host of different languages, to find or develop similar generating procedures. Philip Terry's work thus joins those of Calvino, Mathews, Monk, Helmle, Pastior, and many others as an example of the deep power of literal constraint to force out of otherwise inhibited and restricted imaginations precisely that which the individual, and no one else, has to say.

It is not really necessary to know which letters are missing from which of these nine tales. Indeed, it is probably better to forget entirely that they have been written under constraint. What they say is what they say, however they are written. For the debate that is far from being closed even today, and which has divided Oulipians since the inception of the group, is whether the generating procedure really belongs to the text once it is done, or whether it should rather be treated as a builder treats his scaffold, to be put away in the backyard once the work is finished. It is uncommonly hard to read a text in strict form in both ways at once; but the reassuring thing is that if you read these stories well, without seeking to pin down the rule that controls each one, you will still be aware of the hidden hand of form shaping the expression, and the unique, sad, funny, and stylish world it conveys.

DAVID BELLOS

I'm sorry. The bachelors are the bachelors.

(Herbert Molderings,
The Definitively Unfinished Marcel Duchamp)

PC

LOT

PC ("Slim") Soloman was sitting in a half-full parking lot in his plain black Mason. His radio, on FM 88.5, was off, and by his foot lay a pack of corn biscuits and a lamb tikka sandwich, in clingfilm. His window was partly down, as if for a dog. Out back, a grinding sound, as of a trash truck.

STRIP

PC Soloman took out a strip of pink card which his boss had put in his box two days ago: WATCH BLOCK LOG COMINGS AND GO-INGS. It was a straightforward task, as such things go, possibly too straightforward. PC Soloman wasn't going to complain. Nobody did if on scan duty, it was a day out, away from HQ. Compliant to a worn-out tradition, PC Soloman put this strip into his mouth, and quickly ground it to a pulp with his molars. Having fully wound down his window, PC Soloman now spat it out, onto a patch of asphalt.

BLOCK

This curious building—known as "S" Block, or simply "Ship"—was an award-winning construction on 6 floors, product of a multinational collaboration, involving top brains from Scotland, Norway, Finland, Paraguay and Italy. It was originally put up for a group of naval staff who had rapidly quit it on finding its innovations lacking in comfort. Built with a nod to naval tradition, from various positions its form brought to mind similarly various things of naval origin: a mast, a sail, a buoy, an anchor, a plank, a ship. Its plimsoll mark was at floor 3, half-way up, a thick horizontal band of black paint.

MILK

A milkman doing his round put 10 pints down by "S" Block's big glass front door, took a pad from his coat and did his sums. PC Soloman now saw him post a small bill, and an instant on jump back in his milk cart, continuing his round. PC Soloman took out his biro and log: 08.00 HRS MILKMAN NOTHING SUSPICIOUS.

RUMOUR

Rumour at HQ had it that this block was host to a child porn scam. CID, it was said, had on a standard inquiry found that it was a known origin of illicit 0898s. CID had also found that ads in shop windows for ADULT PHOTOGRAPHY GIRLS (NO MINORS) took cops again to this block. A 2nd rumour had it that a man who had links with a vicious mugging gang had a pad on its top floor. A fotofit of this man was on display at HQ.

LIGHTS

A light was put on in a window of a 3rd floor flat, illuminating its surrounding plimsoll mark. Through a gap in its curtains, PC Soloman saw a woman with dark hair in a pink kimono, standing, hands on hips, waiting for a bit of toast to pop up. Now a light was put on in a 5th floor flat, in which a tall skinny man in black stood smoking, nonchalantly. Again a light was put on at a 3rd floor window, and now 2 on ground floor right. Curtains swung apart, razors cut off facial hair, soaps slid into bath tubs, doors sprang ajar, all around commotion stood in for calm.

TWO-WAY

A two-way radio burst into action, giving out a harsh crackling sound. Against this background a string of staccato cop jargon struck up.

–*Brown Fox to Pink Soloman outcall looking for link-up now. Turn.*
–Pink Soloman to Brown Fox link-up harmony. Turn.
–*Mushrooming task 47, any action 51? Turn.*
–Cool start 51 black frost but long chalk in offing. Turn.
–*59 hot bun continuing black frost radio. Turn.*
–Will do. Turn.
–*Tango. Turn and off.*

Again this harsh crackling sound of PC Soloman's two-way radio as background until it sinks to a buzzing.

CORN

Hungry, PC Soloman took up a pack of corn biscuits lying by his foot. Invitingly, for 6 days, this virgin pack had sat at WPC ("Tiny") Brown's workspot. Now, WPC Brown was sunning a slim brown body on Majorca's sands, following matrimony with PC ("Baldy")

Gray. PC Soloman found it disappointing that such promising biscuits had so quickly got soft. Still, PC Soloman was too hungry to worry about it, much.

TUBA

A musician in black with a tuba in his arm quit "S" Block by its big glass door, taking a path to his right. This door swung shut only to swing back again straight away, disgorging a young woman with fair hair in brown tights and a small child in a Batman suit, who ran haphazardly around a patch of grass in front of "Ship." His mum had a small mouth scar, as if from a fight. Knowing in a flash that this scar was familiar, but not managing to pin this familiarity down, not managing to find its origin, PC Soloman was caught short. This woman was both known and unknown, familiar and unfamiliar. PC Soloman took out his biro and log: 11.30 HRS MUSICIAN OUT WOMAN AND CHILD OUT NOTHING SUSPICIOUS.

DOG

A dog ran across a road, barking at this small child in his Batman suit. His mum told it to piss off if it didn't want a good hiding, making to hit it with a black plastic handbag. It ran away, past "S" Block, into a park. Woman and child took a path off right.

TIKKA

Still hungry following his corn biscuits PC Soloman took up his lamb tikka sandwich which similarly lay by his foot. Taking off its clingfilm PC Soloman saw that a nail on his right hand was partly off, as was his sandwich. Biting into it PC Soloman was hit by its sour odour and, turning towards his fully wound down window, spat a mouthful of lamb tikka out of it. Following this his sandwich was thrown out also, landing on a patch of asphalt.

PINT

A passing youth, stopping unsuspiciously, took hold of a pint of milk and put it in his bag. From a ground floor window a woman took stock of his action. A curtain was rapidly drawn and, an instant on, this woman, on coming out, took in 4 pints of milk. As this passing youth was now out of sight, our woman did not shout at him. PC Soloman took out his log: 12.30 HRS WOMAN OUT AND IN NOTHING SUSPICIOUS.

SCISSORS

PC Soloman took out a pair of scissors which sat on his dashboard, to clip his nail. That vicious mugging gang, thought PC Soloman, had brought scissors into action in an attack. An angry daily, writing this story up, had said: SCISSOR SCANDAL MUST STOP. That was his job, thought PC Soloman. But how was a man to stop such a gang without additional aid? PC Soloman's nail slid out of sight, by his boot.

SKIRT

A woman with pink hair, in a black mini-skirt with pink tights, got out of a cab and, having paid, ran towards "S" Block's big glass door. Looking quickly in a bag, this woman now put a firm thumb on a button and slid through "Ship" 's door. PC ("Slim") Soloman took out his biro and log: 12.45 HRS WOMAN IN SUSPICIOUS.

CONDITIONAL

His two-way radio burst into action again, giving out its usual crackling sound. Against this crackling background staccato cop jargon struck up.

–*Brown Fox to Pink Soloman outcall looking for link-up. Turn.*
–Pink Soloman to Brown Fox link-up harmony. Turn.
–*Continuing hot bun 59, additionals wanting, anything to show 51? Turn.*
–Block in motion, frost mayhow thaw, ask continuing scan. Turn.
–*Grant continuing scan on conditional. Turn.*
–OK. Turn.
–*Tango. Turn and off.*

Again, a crackling sound of his radio until it sinks to a buzzing.

SPURT

PC Soloman took from within his dashboard stow-away a copy of *Spurt*, which his boss had put in his box two days ago, along with his strip of pink card. According to rumour at HQ *Spurt* had links with "S" Block's porn scam. On its front was a monthly gift, a small C30 boasting pornographic chit-chat. Tammy and Cathy await your lust, it said. PC Soloman, scrutinising its glossy colour shots, found that *Spurt*, not unsurprisingly, was full of thighs, tits, backs, bottoms, arms, armpits, hands and smiling happy mouths of girls in shiny birthday suits. PC Soloman found his hand moving onto his groin. No, not on duty, thought PC Soloman.

LIMP

A tall musician in black, carrying a piccolo, quit "S" Block by its big glass door. His piccolo was unusual in that it was gold in colour. It was also unusual in that it was not in its box, but in his hand. This tall musician had a limp. PC Soloman took out his log and biro: 14.00 HRS MUSICIAN OUT NOTHING SUSPICIOUS.

BOLT

PC Soloman took out a bill-fold to look at his cash flow situation. Counting 4 x £5.00 and 2 x £10.00 bills, his curiosity was caught by a tatty photograph of a smart young woman with fair hair, WPC ("Tiny") Brown. PC Soloman had got this photograph from WPC Brown's CV 26 months ago, on WPC Brown's first day at work. Won by a fairy charm, PC Soloman had instantly got a crush on WPC ("Tiny") Brown, along with all 170 odd PCs at HQ, who had for too long had no glamour to lift long and dull days at work. Both ways Cupid's bolt shoots at random: on this occasion, PC ("Baldy") Gray was in luck.

SHADOWS

On "S" Block's 5th floor our woman with pink hair was looking out of a window, touching its glass with a hand. For an instant PC Soloman thought that this woman was motioning to him, in supplication. A curtain was rapidly drawn, by a man. Onto this drawn curtain, owing to bright lights within, its occupants' forms cast long sinuous shadows.

DRAUGHT

PC Soloman took a flask containing hot Bovril from a slot in his door and, pouring a cupful, drank it down. This hot liquid ran gurgling towards his far from full stomach. Tasty, thought PC Soloman, pouring an additional cupful and smacking his lips. For as far as PC Soloman could think back Bovril had had no difficulty in topping his list of hot drinks. Hot soup was good too, now and again, but Bovril was his usual, particularly on days out. Finishing his draught, PC Soloman put his flask back in its slot.

FM

PC Soloman put his radio on from which sounds of a brass band playing "Danny Boy" burst forth, drowning out PC Soloman's rumbling stomach. Twiddling a knob through cross station buzzing to FM 92, playing an aria from Faust, and on to FM 96.5, playing traditional jazz by Bo Mungo, PC Soloman sought randomly for a station to his liking. Stopping for an instant at FM 99 PC Soloman was told in RP of a man's brutal collaring by cops in Dubai for filming of a woman's thighs in sight of an angry husband. This husband was asking for "total support of law." On FM 104 PC Soloman was told all about a Mcdonald's Youth Draw, and on FM 105 Cliff Richard sang a song about not marrying. FM 106 to 108 supplying nothing, PC Soloman put his radio off.

WINDMILL

Our young woman with fair hair and a scar ran towards "S" Block's glass door from its right in pursuit of that naughty child in his Batman suit, who was waving his arms about in a windmill fashion. For an instant, PC Soloman thought Batboy was an unhappy victim of a muscular spasm. A man in a brown shirt and a cap now quit "S" Block, looking anxiously at this show. Batboy's mum caught him by his arm, thrusting him in through "S" Block's door, away from this nosy man. That woman was both known and unknown, thought PC Soloman, familiar and unfamiliar. PC Soloman took out his log and biro: 16.30 HRS WOMAN AND CHILD IN MAN OUT NOTHING SUSPICIOUS.

LIGHTS

All in a flash 4 lights got put on on "S" Block's 3rd floor, and an instant on a 5th light, on its 2nd floor. At a lit window of a flat a man was putting on his coat, whistling with a passion, as if a good night out lay in front of him. PC Soloman had not caught "S" Block's lights going off, during his vigilant day, but saw now it was almost dark. Nights drawing in, thought PC Soloman, turning up his coat collar.

CHIPS

Taking off his cap and quitting his Mason's warmth, PC Soloman got a portion of cod and chips and took it back to his car. This fish and chip shop had a growing standing, mostly on account of its locally caught fish and its bright look. It was run by an Asian, an Asian unafraid of tackling this British national dish. It also did Indian cooking, including many tandoori viands and a host of Pakistani puddings with or without custard. PC Soloman was fond of its onion rings, also.

BROAD

Back in his car PC Soloman took a C30 from *Spurt* and put it on. This C30 had a warning at its start saying that it was only fit for adults with a broad mind. PC Soloman's IQ was 103, which was fairly broad. An instant on and a bubbly sounding woman was talking volubly about how to obtain an orgasm using various kinds of fruit including figs, bananas, passion fruit, kiwi, blackcurrants and corn, which was not a fruit at all. Following this was a kind of hiatus of soft focus music and an additional warning. An instant on and an Irish woman was inviting PC Soloman to unbutton his pants and asking him if sucking action was to his liking, smacking lips, cooing oohs and aahs and isn't it bigs. PC Soloman took hold of a big soggy chip and put it to his lips.

KOMUNGO

Four musicians in black carrying variously a violin, a cor anglais, a Spanish guitar and a komungo quit "S" Block by its big glass door, taking a path to its right. For an instant a sound of hip-hop music burst out from a passing car, diminishing as it shot by. PC Soloman took out his biro and log: 17.10 HRS MUSICIANS OUT NOTHING SUSPICIOUS.

STRIP

A light was put on on "S" Block's 4th floor and right away our young woman with brown tights and scar was standing at a window, closing it. For an instant, this woman stood with curtains framing a slim body in such a way that it was as if on display. Now it was that his first confrontation with this woman at last burst into PC Soloman's mind. On a distant day, that of PC ("Baldy") Gray's stag party, PC Soloman had wound up at a local strip club at which this woman was its 3rd act. Looking up PC Soloman saw his woman drawing thick curtains.

JOB LOT

"S" Block's big glass door swung outwards and an official-looking man in a dark coat put out a job lot of full bin bags, just at that spot at which milk was put that morning. This job lot of bin bags struck ground with a clanging sound, as if full of iron. PC Soloman took up his biro and log: 17.30 HRS JANITOR OUT AND IN NOTHING SUSPICIOUS.

HARMONY

PC Soloman's two-way radio burst into action again, giving out its usual harsh crackling sound. Against this background a string of staccato cop jargon struck up.

–*Brown Fox to Pink Soloman outcall looking for link-up now. Turn.*
–Pink Soloman to Brown Fox link-up harmony. Turn.
–*Full hot bun 59, all outposts on stand-by. Any action 51? Turn.*
–Still frosty 51, no action afoot. Turn.
–*Command swift withdrawal, join 59 additional. Turn.*
–OK. Turn.
–*Tango. Turn and off.*

Again, this crackling sound of PC Soloman's radio until it sinks to a buzzing.

LOT

A pink sports car swung into PC Soloman's lot, pulling up by his black Mason. Sitting in it was a young man in a suit with a young woman who had black lipstick on, and a matching scarf round a mass of black hair, which was in a bun. Stopping his motor and placing his hand on this young woman's lap, this flirty young man put his radio on. On it a man was talking about a dollar fluctuation and its impact on Britain. Straight away now, this young man and woman got snogging, hands and arms participating fully. PC Soloman, starting his Mason and shifting it into 1st, put his foot down. Off, thought PC Soloman, and was.

COPY-WRITER

After the takeover by the Aphrodite conglomerate all articles had to be on sex. In the old days we'd done articles on pottery, fishing, tennis, cars, more or less everything in a word. Now we only did sex. We were still able to cover topics like cars, certainly, yet we had to do it from a sexy *angle*. Vintage cars were no go, leggy blondes on bonnets were in.

TESCO'S

If in search of a partner, don't despair. Remember: there are plenty of available women at large, and tracking them down won't be hard. It can be enjoyable too. The aisles at Tesco's are as good a place as any to begin talent-spotting: normally there's always something very tasty on display. A man in search of a lover can look nowhere better. Rich rewards are certain. As bees fill parks and playing fields, hovering over the clover, bobbing from dandelion to dandelion, so girls swarm to Tesco's in crowds.

As redactor of the poetry section I was a bit miffed at first. How was I to do *poetry* from a sexy angle? *N'importe!* Then I had one of my brainwaves, fairly predictable, perhaps, yet it felt like a brainwave at the time: I'd do a weekly selection of *love* poetry. What simpler! I sat down excitedly at my PC and concocted a list of likely candidates, from Sappho to Tony Harrison, shook the lot into alphabetical order (no problem for the Whipp-IT) and *voilà!* There it was: my next six months' work completed in seconds. I was feeling rather pleased with myself, zesty, so I resolved to nip over to the *Café Sélavy* for a light snack. I gave Di a bell to see if she'd come along— she wasn't interested for some reason or other. Afterwards, a little heady, I called in to speak with the new editor, Gross.

IMAGE

People say that dress is very important here, and in a way they're right. Yet try not to be one of those who spend a lot of time in front of the mirror or who stick pots of gel in their hair. A nice pair of jeans and a good shirt is all that's needed. Nothing too fancy. There's no harm in getting one's hair done at a good salon, yet don't waste time with hair-spray or wax. Leave that to the ladies. Above all a man needs to keep himself clean. Wash the back and face properly to avoid spots—and don't forget the genitals.

When I left the editor's office I was cross. Very cross. I was *fâché*. In brief, his lordship wasn't interested in my project—he had plans of his own he said. Poetry was to be axed—it had no mass market appeal—and he wanted me to deliver a new weekly slot, anything I liked so long as it was sexy. Like some latter-day Gradgrind he wanted facts, not fiction, and he wanted them fast: dismissing me he gave me till the end of the week to present my draft. I was indignant, for I'd taken a certain pride in the poetry section, had even, I felt, commanded an appreciable readership. What was happening to the world, I wondered? I'd hand in my notice and decamp.

EMAIL

Too mannered a style is likely to repel the girls, so take care. Write in an everyday manner, with familiar yet well-chosen words. If she rejects the message, sends it back at once, press on—she may look at it later. Time breaks intractable oxen, teaches schoolboys to do homework. There is nothing as soft as water, nothing as hard as stone: yet the constant dripping of water hollows the hardest granite. Keep sending messages—in the end, with perseverance, she'll be won over. To begin with she might send back angry notes, protesting "Lay off, for God's sake!" Yet what she wants, what she really really wants, is for the messages to keep coming. Press hard, at the end of the day that's the only way to win.

On reflection I decided not to give in so easily. I didn't want Gross to have too facile a victory. I'd take him on. I'd write his sordid slot if it was the last thing I did. I sat myself in front of the Whipp-IT, took hold of my pipe and waited for inspiration to come. After a short while my pipe lay dormant and I'd made no progress. My mind was a blank, as was the screen of the Whipp-IT. *Anything I liked so long as it was sexy.* I didn't see myself as an Agony Alec, nor did I wish to mastermind an interminable series of confessional-style interviews with men on their bedroom habits. Ben Bishop, 35. Head of Foreign Exchange at P. K. Marks. Has slept with more than 95 women. I'd have been interested in a piece on changing libidinal mores in the West, starting with the Greeks. Yet this might take a lot of work and Gross still find it lacking. Then I had a better idea.

SKILL

In love as in all else, skill is indispensable. The skill-less man won't get anywhere. Whether one is in search of a steady relationship or simply a good night on the town, skill will be needed. As the saying goes, skill and confidence are a winning team. Skill can control love itself. Many people, when they're in the mood, simply dive in and don't think twice. And, certainly, there's a lot to be said for spontaneity. Yet if a man has skill on his side, there'll be a proportionately greater chance of reaping the greatest rewards from the occasion when it arises.

I'd been wrestling with Ovid's *Ars Amatoria* in the evenings. On and off I'd been working on a translation, yet it wasn't really coming together as I'd have wished. What if I were to redirect this project and present it—in prose—as my slot? I'd have to take a few liberties with the original, certainly, even stray into the realms of *free-translation* if I were to get away with it, yet despite my reservations on these matters the project had an irresistible appeal. Firstly, it kept me in work—it gave me a theme. Secondly, it acted as my secret revenge on Gross. He'd never spot the trick, so the joke was going to be on him. In this way the project kept a roof over my head and threatened the stability of the roof over his. What better?

DOGS

Go to the dogs: the broad arena offers loads of openings. Here there's no need of secret finger-talk, private signals, nods and winks: stand right next to the woman who's most attractive, breathe down her neck, give her a winning smile. Then invent some reason to start a conversation—anything will do. Ask who owns those dogs trotting by: discover her preferred canine, then back it later on. If some lager spills on her dress, wipe it off. If her coat's trailing, grab it, make a great to-do of saving it from the dirt. Instant reward for gallantry: a licensed peep at perfectly formed ankles, and more.

On my way home from the office I dove into a little second-hand bookshop I knew to grab any versions of the Ovid they might have— they were very obliging, had three. Took me for a scholar—at my age! I set to work that evening, preferring not to commence the project in the office in case my constant looting of Ovid's *Ars* seemed odd. To start with I re-read the poem from start to finish, to refresh my sense of its overall design. I decided rapidly that I'd have to concentrate on books 1 and 2 which gave advice to men on where and how to catch a mate. Book 3, with its advice to women, was inappropriate for a men's magazine. Having in this way narrowed down my target, I looked more closely at the first two books, jotting down any ideas in the margin as I went. So as to avoid anachronism I allowed myself to change the locale when necessary: there was no point sending my readers to the woodland shrine of Diana near Aricia. Similarly, I saw few prospects for javelins and chariots. And I let myself play with the order of the poem whenever necessary.

SEASON

It's a mistake to imagine that only ferry companies and farmers need pay attention to the season. Grain cannot always be committed to the disloyal soil, nor bow doors to the ball-shrinking sea. Similarly it's not always wise to chase girls; the occasion will often condition the victory. Times to avoid are:

BIRTHDAYS
BREAKDOWNS
DIETS
DRIVING TESTS
EXAMS
LOTTERY WINS
PERIODS
PERMS

There are certainly others too—it will pay to keep a list, adding to it when occasion arises. Never make a move at these times. Best sit tight: those who set sail at the wrong moment hobble home with a dismembered vesicle.

Pretty soon I'd arranged my data by heading, and I set to work translating this information into blocks of prose. The voice which emerged was neither Ovid's—even if it shared his cynicism at times—nor my own, yet rather that of a different persona altogether: a species of lecher-come-man-of-the-world for the most part, yet not entirely. The whole enterprise was very T-in-C, yet I tried to work at the tone till this wasn't too transparent. Finally, when I felt I'd hit the mark, I showed these early drafts to Gross.

TIMING

Timing might be seen as part of skill, yet I give it a separate entry since it has a bearing on more aspects of love than performance alone. Timing is as important when dating as in the sack. Even in those first moments of a nascent relationship, when a man doesn't know whether it's game on or game off, timing is of the essence. In order to break into a conversation with the object of desire, it doesn't really matter what's said, it's more important to say it at the right

time, so as to get heard. Keep an eye on her, while ogling the competi-
tion, wait till her friend's gone to the toilets. That's the moment to
make a move: sitting on her own she'll have her defences down. Tak-
ing the seat next to her pay attention to bearing—she'll be more inter-
ested in looks than anything else at this stage. And where opening
lines are concerned remember the importance of first impressions.
Don't say anything too corny.

This time, it seemed, I'd got it right. Not only did Gross approve the
project, he positively gave it his benison. He even praised its moder-
nity! *La vache!* We agreed SEX-TIPS as an apposite title, and he
allowed me to present the pieces beneath the aegis of a pen-name.
VOID'S SEX-TIPS was destined to start the following week. It was
all stations go.

EXERCISE

The importance of exercise can't be stressed too strongly. Exercise of
the whole body. Try going jogging twice a week. And go swimming
too if at all possible. The swimming pool is an ideal place for talent-
spotting as well, a chance to get a good look at what's on offer in the
area. If swimming doesn't appeal, there are plenty of alternatives
which will do: archery, tennis, allball, golf, anything at all. In the
case of golf, don't neglect the nineteenth hole. Like the swimming
pool, it's a good place for talent-spotting, especially if older women
appeal. Avoid snooker, however, darts too, and above all avoid going
to the gym. It won't help to be smelling of smoke and beer, nor is there
any point spending time somewhere that doesn't allow mingling.
Many gyms now hold women only sessions, so be warned. Whatever
one's personal preference, however, it's exercise which is the key.

Take-off went well and my slot seemed to go from strength to
strength over the first few weeks. Gross was very pleased with the
general response. Men all over were pleased, he said, it was the sort
of thing they'd been wanting to hear for a long time. It was so fresh.
We even had some letters asking VOID'S advice on specific sex-re-
lated problems. How important was length? What was to be done
with smelly feet? There was, indeed, little on the down side, only
one acescent and incognito fax: F*** VOID.

COMPLEXION

Let every lover be pale: this is the proper complexion for love. Only
an anaemic look will do the trick. Try TOTAL BLOCK—don't be
tempted by parasols.

After the keenness of the initial response, to stop things from flag-ging, Gross had some T-shirts printed, which were given away to selected readers. FOLLOW THE VOID. VOID IS LOVE. My slot be-came widely talked over in many circles, even if the T-shirts didn't make the front page of *Paris Match*, yet I kept wondering when someone was going to blow my cover. This, after all, had been my initial plan—so as to embarrass Gross—yet as week followed week, and soon weeks slipped into months, nobody seemed to notice the deceit. Void became the talk of the town, while Ovid rolled over in his grave.

DRINK

A word of warning is called for on the matter of drink. Keep the mind clear and the feet steady. Above all avoid drinkers' brawls, never get into a fight when it can be avoided. Drink of an evening was intended to promote high spirits and games. Yet while excess can be damaging, to act pissed can help. Stammer words and roll eyeballs, then however sex-laden the speech, it'll be blamed on the booze. This way she can get to know what the man within really thinks of her. And if it backfires—booze is to blame.

One day I met Di for a bite at the *Café Sélavy*. I remember the occa-sion distinctly, for the place was teeming with workmen. Almost immediately she mentioned VOID. I was certain she was going to mention Ovid too, and blow my cover. After all, she had a degree in Classical Civilization, albeit from a Polyversity. Yet I was mistaken. With *acharnement*, she went into an endless diatribe on sexism and sexploitation, charging my magazine with being reactionary, spoke of complicity with the backlash against feminism. I said nothing. It was clear that Di, and many other women in her office, if she were to be believed, reckoned VOID'S SEX-TIPS extremely OFFENSIVE. She finished off by asking me if I'd do something to stop it. Told me it was my obligation, as a NEW MAN. I was deeply embarrassed, yet said I'd do anything in my power.

FEET

No girl I have ever met has been attracted by smelly feet. Yet this is no reason for a man to be ashamed if he's the sweaty type—he can see this as part of his maleness. As long as it never gets beyond control. There are plenty of good deodorants on the market which can solve the general problem. Personally, I stick to "Thor," it has a strong male image and not too potent a smell; however, there are plenty of other

brands to choose from which are as good. Where looks are concerned,
don't neglect footwear. Many women maintain that one can tell a
man by his shoes. Yet don't be misled by this: it doesn't pay to be too
showy. It's best to avoid extremes, like cowboy boots and sandals.
Slip-ons are a safe bet.

The following day at work I revised the forthcoming SEX-TIPS on
the Whipp-IT, toning them down if anything, with deference to Di.
For example, I remember deleting a passage on the flabby stomachs
and backsides of older women. Later, I took the machine on at chess,
beginners' level. People had the impression I was working, while in
reality I was playing chess; or being beaten at chess, it came to the
same thing between myself and the Whipp-IT.

PRESENTS

Don't be too lavish with presents—anyone can win over a lover that
way, yet they'll soon have their pockets emptied. A gift held back
breeds expectations, and if one can contrive to catch her present-free,
she'll keep on giving in case she loses what she's already given. Every
girl knows how to fleece a desperate man. When she's in a mood for
spending she'll take him to the shops, ask him to inspect the mer-
chandise, give his expert opinion. She'll give him a snog, then insist
he pay for it, swear it'll really satisfy her, insist she have it right now,
that she really really needs it. No, tricks like this are to be avoided. A
sensible man has to tell her at the beginning he's skint, that he's be-
tween jobs, that money can't win love. That way, even if she lets him
down, at least he won't be the worse off.

There was an easing off at work for a few days after this, leaving
plenty of time for me to get beaten at chess by the Whipp-IT, time
and again. In the end, lighting my pipe, I resorted to watching the
Whipp-IT play itself, *beat* itself, which gave me a certain sadistic
thrill. One day, I was alarmed to find two letters among my corre-
spondence which took VOID to task. One was a complaint from a
chap who'd tried to accost a woman in Tesco's and finished with getting ejected by the store detectives—they had the whole thing on
CCTV and were going to press charges. The other was from a
woman, and complained that EMAIL was sexist.

WATERFALLS

Waterfalls, whether or not accompanied by the added boon of a
nearby mill, are romantic places, and their isolation can be handy.
Here a man may chance on a maiden on her own. If she's to his fancy,

it's okay to bring force to bear—force like that always goes down a
treat with the women. Indeed, what they'd love to give freely, they'd
really prefer to have stolen. Coarse love-making drives them wild,
the boldness of near-rape excites them—and the woman who was al-
most forced into sex, yet managed to get away, while she may feign
relief, in reality feels disappointed. If things get problematic after-
wards, don't worry. Let's face it, only the base gives delight; men seek
only their own enjoyment, and find added joy when this comes from
another's pain.

It was company policy at this time to ignore complaints, so we did.
As Gross said, what was the point in being a writer if nobody ever
got offended? We gave both letters the scissors treatment. Regrettably, while we had no way of foreseeing this, these first written complaints were only the thin end of the wedge. As the days went by, to
great alarm, the complaints grew and grew and ignoring them became correspondingly harder and harder. Typical complaints relied
heavily on the word "sexist;" others complained of "macho ethics,"
the denigration of "woman-as-object;" some bemoaned VOID'S
"phallocentrism."

OLDER WOMEN

If she's no spring chicken and already applying anti-wrinkle creams
and tinting her hair don't ask her date of birth—leave this sort of
thing to the Passport Office. Women of this age-bracket and above
are well worth it. Moreover, they have experience and know-how on
their side, and compensate for their age with art, concealing their
years with expensive powders and ointments. Best of all, they have a
million positions for the sack, many more than The Joy of Sex *con-*
tains. For novices, new bottled wine; for me, a vintage that has rip-
ened over the years. Does anybody disbelieve me? Take me at my
word, I promise satisfaction.

Complaints peaked after the appearance of VOID on WATER-
FALLS. The piece was seen—with a certain logic, granted—as an
incitement to rape. Recent statistics had shown that rape was on
the rise again, and VOID, along with several readily available video
nasties, was targeted as an IMPORTANT FACTOR. We received an
avalanche of mail, containing several letters from prominent femi-
nists, and another acescent and incognito fax: F*** VOID.

AVAILABILITY

Always remember, every girl can be trapped. Any man can catch a

*bird if he sets his nets right. Swallows will more readily cease their
singing in spring, than a keen lover's entreaties fail with a single
girl. Why do men not acknowledge that they can win any woman in
sight? Few indeed are those who respond with a no, and whether or
not they're game, an amatory proposition is something they all cher-
ish. And if she doesn't take the bait, rejection carries no shame. Yet
how can rejection follow when joys delight? What we don't possess
has ever more charm than what we do. The grass is always greener
in another man's garden, the herd over the road has fatter teats.*

Before we knew it we were swarmed by libbers. It was like
Greenham Common all over again. When we kicked them from the
foyer, they took root on the stairs. When we kicked them off the
stairs, they camped by the front door, not for an instant ceasing to
rail at their attackers: "Fascist bastards!" "Alien aggressors!" "Men!"
We were forced to call the police in, to keep the peace, and soon the
parking lot was swarming with Panda cars and black Masons. The
women carried banners.

VOID=RAPE

AVOID VOID

OPENING GAMBITS

*Avoid things like "Does madam come here often?" or "Haven't we met
somewhere before?" If it's appropriate, ask her if she'd like a drink,
or, if she's a smoker, whether she'd like a cigarette. This way, before
committing himself, a man can get her talking and form some impression as to her character. A lot can be decided in those first few
moments, so it's best to take one's time. And even after the romance is
off the mark, when he's been going steady with her for two or three
weeks, what a man says is still very important. Is it the moment to
give her a French kiss? The time to reach for her breasts? This kind of
decision, certainly, is finally in the hands of the party concerned,
and is dependent on a lot of criteria. Yet whatever decision is
reached, be certain to make the move with the help of an appropriate
opening gambit.*

Soon the libbers had pitched their tents in the fields opposite. It
was going to be a friendly protest, they said. They lit bonfires and
toasted tea-cakes, forever playing their cheap banjos, chanting

their inane slogans:

> VOID spells RAPE
> to every girl,
> so say Sally, Jane
> and Shirl!

It was not my idea of a *fête champêtre*. It became impossible to concentrate at the office, and there was a bad atmosphere.

APHRODISIACS

There are plenty of aphrodisiacs on the market these days, from Spanish Fly to Danish Egg, all sold on their bedding-power. My advice is steer clear. Giving aphrodisiacs to women can be a real danger: they can interfere with the brain and promote schizophrenia. Nasty tricks of this kind are to be avoided. To get a lover a man needs to prove himself loveable, and this cannot be achieved by good looks alone. If he wants to try aphrodisiacs himself, he might go for those which spring from mother earth herself. Eat white onions and colewort, enrich the diet with avocados, honey, and the tasty kernels of the pine tree.

While everybody else at the office was negotiating with the police and the libbers, trying to end the protest, I was becoming increasingly concerned that my cover might be blown, that someone might bring Ovid into the debate. In a way my worries were hypocritical, yet at the same time that I wanted my trick to be discovered—in the end—I was enjoying my work in a way I hadn't for years; so I didn't relish the prospect of being laid off, which was inevitable if a revelation came. As it happened, I need not have worried as I did. For while the crisis was receiving ever-increasing media attention, and people started associating themselves with one side or other of the debate, the exiled Roman poet was never mentioned. As Ovid himself said, anticipating one of the moderns by over 1900 years: "Poetry, I fear, is held in small esteem."

SEASON

Never forget the importance of season. As there are bad times to strike, so there are good. These often fall immediately after positive or negative events, so be alert. Be on the watch for some of these:

BEREAVEMENTS
BIRTHDAYS

DIETS
EXAMS
FESTIVALS
HOLIDAYS
LOTTERY WINS
PERIODS
SEPARATIONS
SHOPPING SPREES

These are only a few ideas to be going along with—it'd be easy to add to the list. These really are the best moments at which to strike. If a man sets sail now, he'll come home to port with swollen nets.

The libbers carried on toasting their tea-cakes and playing their cheap banjos, waving their banners and chanting their slogans. Things at work became tense: nobody was able to concentrate on what they were doing and it became impossible to meet important deadlines. Gross was always in a shitty mood, and while he was adamant that we had to stick to principles, that we weren't going to give an inch to these lesbian vagrants, his temper flew in my direction more often than not. To make matters worse, the media debate was swinging more and more against the magazine, against VOID, and sales, which had soared in the first weeks of the protest, had now dropped to an all time low. Gross was not happy, and, increasingly, I felt like a pariah.

POETRY

Nobody cares for poetry. Girls aren't interested—they prefer expensive presents. Any ignorant blockhead can catch their attention provided he's wealthy. Today really is the Golden Age: gold gets friends, position and love. If Byron dropped in—accompanied by the Graces, yet short of cash—he'd be shown the door at once. The only time to flatter girls in verse is St. Valentine's day—a bawdy declamation, the trashier the better—this will do to win their love. Sophisticated or plain silly, at these times they'll take a poem fashioned in the early dawn, for them, as a welcome gift.

Things had reached the point where something had to give, and the decision had to be in the hands of Gross. Not only was he editor—indirectly, the whole thing was his creation. If he'd let my selection of love poetry see the light of day the libbers might never have batted an eyelid. One afternoon he called me to his office, solemnly told me I was to take a month's leave. That VOID was to stop, following the appearance of those in press, at least till the crisis blew over. He told me that my job was safe, that personally he rated my work, he even gave me an idea for a new slot I might like to take on, on the sex lives of insects. He wanted me to cover something less controversial. I met Di that day at the *Café Sélavy*. Told her I was going on leave; and of the editor's decision to end the VOID slot. She was delighted—thanked me for my good work, said I was a winner. Evidently, she didn't connect my leave with the VOID affair.

TWO-TIMING

No man can be expected to stick to a single girl. Have a good time by all means, yet act with discretion. Don't boast of affairs simply to boost the ego. If well-hidden affairs are discovered nonetheless, deny them flatly. Never be slavish, don't resort to excessive flattery—to do so is certain proof of wrong-doing. Go for it in the sack, that's the only way to win her over, with a screw so good it eradicates all misgivings.

I was away for a month, in what felt more like exile than leave. I spent some time in Constantinople—I can't bear to call it by its official appellation—visiting the temples and palaces, then spent a week or so on the Black Sea, a desolate, barely habitable region. I sent a few postcards—one to Di depicting the harem at Topkapi—telling people what a great time I was having, and that I wished they were here; yet in reality I was bored to tears, dying to get back to *terra nostra*. The Ottomans are a dreary race, all kilims and cartomancy.

VARIETY

Women's characters are all different. To trap twenty hearts calls for twenty different methods. Some soils are best for barley, some for oats, and some for rye: they can't all be grown in the same field. Women have as many altering roles as the protean gods. One needs to adapt oneself as occasion demands, to transform oneself, like the shape-changer, into water, then a horse, now a dog, a hog, a headless bear, sometime a fire. Some fish are got by trawling, some with nets, some with line and hook. Above all, don't attempt the same method on all age-brackets: an old bird will spot the nets from afar.

When I got back things had altered irrevocably, as if by some bizarre sea change. There were no tents opposite the office block, no chanting femos. Traffic was flowing normally. There were no Panda cars, no black Masons. When I went into the office—*C'est pas pos-*

sible!—it was no longer *there*. After the initial shock, one of the porters told me we'd been relocated onto floor 18. Here, I was greeted by the new editor, Goodman, who welcomed me back with open arms. I'd find editorial policy somewhat changed, he said, now that the Aphrodite conglomerate had gone into receivership. My desk was new—false mahogany—yet the Whipp-IT was still in place. I switched it on. Lit my pipe. Had a few games of chess. Lost. Then I spotted the NO SMOKING sign.

ENDING A RELATIONSHIP

Ending a relationship is never easy, especially if it had some happy moments, yet even the brightest stars fade, and there's always a time when it's best to close shop. An amicable parting is best—don't dash to the bench from the bedroom, and let her hang on to any gifts to avoid litigation. Be pitiless, don't go all soft when she starts to cry— women teach their eyes to sob at will. Silence is strength: the lover who reproaches a girl is inviting her to prove him wrong. Don't give reasons for wanting a separation: foster a grievance, don't give her it in black and white.

The new management regime had a new brief: "Sexy not Sexist." And Goodman gave the go-ahead to my long-cherished selection of love poetry. I battled with *limbo* in the Whipp-IT, emerging the victor in the end, and re-began work on my selection, avoiding Ovid to be on the safe side. I printed some risky pieces, yet the slot proved to be well-liked, giving rise to no protest.

In the end things were resolved fairly satisfactorily. Gross got the boot and I'm still in work. Yet the victory seems hollow somehow, for it took place behind my back. Paradoxically, now, I look back on those days beneath Gross with nostalgia. Yet it still irritates me that nobody spotted my scam.

BUSBOY

1.

Maddy says she's not interested unless you stop smoking. No buts. Maddy used to smoke like a Turk. Now she's stopped and she wants you to stop as well. She wants you to choose between her and smoking. She wants you to choose *her*. Can't we talk about it, you say. Maddy puts the phone down.

2.

You undress a fresh pack of Gitanes, tap the box until one of the line of cigarettes pokes its head above the level of the others. You slip it out, light up, inhale.

3.

Nothing could be clearer. Either you give up the fags for Maddy, or you give up Maddy for the fags. The problem is you want both; you want to be *spoilt*. You want Maddy *and* the fags.

4.

You take out another cigarette. Light it. Inhale.

5.

At the café they ask if you've seen Maddy. You say no, that she's playing hard to get. You clear the tables from lunch in readiness for the next set of customers.

6.

There are two ways out of the dilemma as you see it. You either travel back in time looking for Maddy-who-still-smokes-like-a-Turk (difficult); or you persuade Maddy to re-start (also difficult, but less so). Other ways out you will consider later.

7.

"A cigarette is the perfect type of perfect pleasure. It is delicious, and it leaves one unsatisfied. What more can one want?"—Oscar Wilde.

8.

From a call box you phone the Smokers' Helpline. You ask them how you should go about preventing a friend from stopping. As soon as they have understood your demand they hang up.

9.

That evening you take a long meditative bath. You smoke a joint, then suture the remaining Gitanes. Before going to bed you drink a large tumbler of whisky accompanied by a Havana cigar. You dream of Maddy, smoking.

10.

At the café there are workmen installing a waterwheel propelled by an artificial waterfall. The dust and noise created by their goings on keeps most customers at bay, despite the BUSINESS AS USUAL sign in the window. You sit in a corner reading the daily papers, nursing your sore head with a glass of tonic water.

11.

You phone Maddy. There is nobody at home. When the ansaphone whirrs into action you speak calmly: *call me*.

12.

Later, you check out the smoking section at the local library: predictably, there is a great deal on stopping, nothing on starting up. The only book holding any promise, Richard Klein's *Cigarettes Are Sublime,* you read in one sitting, without stopping for a cigarette. You are particularly impressed by his chapter on *Carmen,* which describes the seductive powers attributed to tobacco in the opera. You resolve to take Maddy to see it.

13.

Outside you light up, taking a profound drag on your cigarette, letting its toxic smoke caress the cilia of your lungs.

14.

You phone Maddy. Still the ansaphone. When it whirrs into action you speak calmly once again: *please.* You flirt with the idea of paying her an impromptu visit. Think better of it. Light up.

15.

> Sweet talk, sweet talk of lovers
>> it's all smoke!
> Their raptures, their raptures, and their vows,
>> it's all smoke!
> Drifting away into the air, we watch
>> the smoke
>> the smoke
>> the smoke
>> the smoke!

—Georges Bizet, *Carmen.*

16.

In the park two small boys are playing on the slides. Behind them, on a bench, sits their young mother, smoking. You ask her for a light.

17.

Your ideal lover.
She would smoke *all the time.*

18.

Maddy phones. She asks if you've given up. You say you've bought two tickets for *Carmen.*

Have you given up?
Will you come, then?
If you've given up.

You lie, say yes, you have. She blows you a kiss down the phone.

19.

You spend an evening in front of the television, smoking Old Holborn. Before turning in you flirt with your pipe over a small port. You dream that someone has stuck pins into your cigarette box, so that when you go for a smoke the cigarettes emerge tattered, flayed.

20.

At the café they ask after Maddy. You say you're meeting her in the evening. That you're going to a show. You clean out the coffee grinders, sweep the floor.

21.

A down-and-out stops you in the street. Asks you for a light. You reach into your pocket and pull out your lighter. Offer it to him. He takes it, pockets it. Then asks you for a cigarette.

22.

In the park three fit-looking men in tracksuits are jogging round the outer path. Sitting on your bench, cigarette in hand, you follow their fictional movements with your gaze. Where are they going?

23.

Your Top Ten.
Gitanes
Gauloises
Lucky Strike ("It's toasted!")
Marlboro
Camel
Benson and Hedges
Rothmans
Navy Cut
JPS
MS

24.

"The healthy are not real. They have everything except *being*— which is only confirmed by uncertain health."—E.M. Cioran.

25.

You weigh up your chances of converting Maddy. Low. Nevertheless, you purchase a packet of Silk Cut, just in case she rises to the bait.

26.

You light a Gitane. Inhale. You exhale slowly, through the nose, the smoke descending in swirling eddies over your lips and chin, enveloping your head in its dizzying cloud.

27.

Maddy arrives late at the opera, and you are shuffled ungraciously into two pillar seats. The production is set on the planet Argon, in the 21st century. Carmen works in a microchip factory. None of the cast smoke, and the songs have been altered accordingly. Nevertheless, after the performance, you offer Maddy a cigarette. I knew you were lying, she says.

28.

You smoke your last cigarette of the day, accompanied by a tumblerful of whisky. When you stub out the cigarette a fair amount of whisky remains. You top it up, smoke another last cigarette of the day.

29.

At the café they ask you about the show. You say it was great, that Maddy loved it too. A fetching young woman with dark hair and prominent breasts asks you for a coffee. You take her order, pass it on, without bothering to explain you're not one of the waiters yourself.

30.

Already, you are beginning to lose hope of converting Maddy. She's a tough nut to crack, and you haven't the necessary stratagems. As a last resort you decide to try getting her pissed.

31.

Your *bête noire*.
NO SMOKING signs.

32.

You telephone Maddy: no reply.

33.

In a bar you find yourself eyeing up the women customers. One girl in particular, wearing pink tights and a tartan mini-skirt, smoking roll-ups, attracts your attention. Before you leave your eyes meet: the look in hers is hostile.

34.

A friend tells you he's seen Maddy with another man. You remark that she's not your property. That she's often to be seen in the company of other men.

35.

"The cigarette is the prayer of our time."—Annie Leclerc.

36.

It occurs to you there might be another way out of your dilemma. Rather than having *Maddy* and the fags, you could have *another woman* and the fags. Even *another-woman-who-smokes-like-a-Turk* and the fags. A compromise, for sure: but better than Maddy plus no fags. An improvement too on fags plus no Maddy.

37.

In bed you toss yourself off, thinking alternately of Maddy and the woman with prominent breasts.

38.

In the café you empty an ashtray full of lipstick-stained cigarettes. You read the Lonely Hearts.

Fit 31yo, brunette. Virgo, hedonist,
seeks 24-30yo Gemini man, GSOH, for
partying etc. NS.—ML 25066.

Woman, WLTM warm, wickedly funny man
for walks, talks and corks. When will
I get my cuddle? NS.—ML 13072.

NS could only mean one of two things: NO SEX or NO SMOKING.

39.

You telephone Maddy. There is nobody at home. When the ansaphone comes on you put down the receiver.

40.

In the park two small boys are playing on the slides. On a bench behind them sits their young mother. You sit down beside her, ask her for a light. She says she's given up.

41.

"The cigarette, which is the most imperious, the most engaging, the most demanding, the most loving, the most refined of mistresses, tolerates nothing which is not her, and compromises with nothing."
—Théodore de Banville.

42.

You light a cigarette. The smoke pierces your lungs, then emerges slowly, softly enfolding your body in its mist, at once extending and dissolving the body's limits, erasing the boundary marking inside and outside.

43.

You phone Maddy. No answer.

44.

You wander from bar to bar in the hope of picking someone up. It's so long since you did this sort of thing that you forget how to read the signs. You get as far as asking for a light three times, but even when the response is encouraging you fail to follow up your first move, retreat to your own table to enjoy the cigarette, your only true mistress. Late in the evening, when you're fairly drunk, you manage to share a few drinks with a student taking a year out. Even though you don't fancy her, at least she smokes. When the bar closes you invite her back to your place. She says no.

45.

You stumble clumsily into bed, hit the light. You dream you are in a forest. At the forest's edge you find a path leading up into the mountains. You climb to the top, where you find a lake. You are about to strip off and go for a swim when, suddenly, snow begins to fall, fast and hard.

46.

At the café you cut the stems off some gladioli with a blunt pair of scissors before placing them in vases on the dining tables. Again, you leaf through the Lonely Hearts. Again, NS everywhere.

47.

A friend tells you you're looking rough. You're *feeling* rough, you say.

48.

You phone Maddy. She picks up the receiver.

Hello?
Hello, Maddy, it's me.
Oh!
I'm sorry, we've got to talk.
About?
Maddy, please, why don't you come round for a drink?
No thanks.
Then can we meet?

Eventually, she agrees. Insists on her place. You assent, not too enthusiastically.

49.

Your worst nightmare.
Finding the 24 hour garage shut.

50.

You buy a packet of Marlboro. Smoke half of them on the trot.

51.

"If Prometheus had stolen fire from heaven in order to light his cigarette, they would have let him do it."—Mme de Girardin.

52.

When you arrive at Maddy's flat she's watching *Casablanca* on TV. You make an ironic remark about allowing Humphrey Bogart to chain-smoke in her sitting room. Regret it. During the meal you keep topping up her wine glass. Every time you do so she smiles at you, in her enchanting, disapproving way. When you've finished eating you casually roll a joint, offer it to Maddy. She refuses, says she has a headache, is going to bed.

53.

You catch the last bus home. Finish off the evening with your remaining cigarettes and a can of beer. You dream you are attacked by an oversized pair of scissors.

54.

You wake up wanting Maddy more than ever. You are mad about her all over again.

55.

Running full tilt in the face of your most powerful instincts, you resolve to STOP.

56.

You telephone Maddy. There is no answer.

57.

At the café you busy yourself placing small brightly coloured paper parasols into slices of melon. You empty an ashtray full of lipstick-stained cigarettes, holding it at arm's length.

58.

In the park you stroll round the outer path, soon becoming breathless. You need a cigarette.

59.

You telephone Maddy. Still no answer.

60.

Your favourite colour.
Blue.

61.

Increasingly in need of a cigarette you visit the local library again to solicit the aid of its literature. *Stop Now!* advises you to begin by disgusting yourself with cigarettes, suggests smoking a *whole* packet. You follow its advice. Then smoke another.

62.

A friend tells you he succeeded with nicotine patches. I'm a new man, he says.

63.

In the evening you smoke your last cigarette. Ever. Four times. You dream someone's fist-fucking your lungs.

64.

You wake with a sore throat, drink a glass of orange juice and chew a clove of garlic. Following the course of action prescribed by *Stop Now!* you free-associate, writing out a list of all that is bad about cigarettes.

THEY KILL YOU
THEY STOP YOU SLEEPING WITH MADDY
THEY KILL YOU
THEY ARE EXPENSIVE
THEY STOP YOU SLEEPING WITH MADDY
THEY KILL YOU
THEY CAUSE BRONCHITIS AND OTHER DISEASES
THEY STOP YOU SLEEPING WITH MADDY
THEY STOP YOU SLEEPING WITH MADDY

65.

In the park there is a juggler practicing. You watch him trying to light his cigarette while maintaining his three batons in the air. He drops one, but is able to scoop it up again with his foot.

66.

From a call box you phone Maddy. There is nobody at home. When the ansaphone whirrs into action you speak forcibly: *call me.*

67.

At the café they ask after Maddy. You shrug. You distribute ashtrays in the smoking area. Breathing in deeply, hugging the margins of the occupied tables, you gather as many fumes into your lungs as passive smoking allows.

68.
A friend offers you a cigarette. You refuse, saying you have stopped.

69.

> Life is a cigarette,
> Cinder, ash, and fire,
> Some smoke it in a hurry,
> Others savour it.
>
> —Manuel Machado

70.

At home you find yourself biting your nails. You tell yourself to stop. You find your hand reaching out for a cigarette. What the hell, you think. A last last cigarette. You light it, inhale.

71.

Maddy phones. Asks if you've stopped. Yes and no, you say.

Meaning?
I'm just smoking my last.
Good.

She asks you to call her in a week if you've still stopped. The deal stands.

72.

That evening you have a cup of tea and a joint, go to bed early. You can't sleep. Get up. Have another cup of tea, another joint. In bed. You wake to find your mattress on fire, heave it out the window, crash on the couch. You dream of Maddy, smoking.

BOOKSELLER

That's the way Blue, you can do it, get that blessed key into the lock old boy, that's the first thing. Rusty old effort's not fit for a brothel if you'll excuse Blue saying so. In fact it's totally *knackered*. Not the only one either. The governor should have had it changed long ago. Ah! There we go. At last! The little bugger. Catch your death standing out here in the street all day. Now, close up again, just until we get the lights on and then sort the place out a bit. See if we can create a little order. Easier said than done in this place, I can assure you, but then beggars can't be choosers. There, at least we can see where we're going now. Christ, there goes the blower already. Who could that be I wonder? After the governor no doubt. I don't know why they bother, he's never in before lunch, they ought to know that. Leave it Blue, leave it. Sorry sir, but we're not open till nine-thirty. It's stopped. Thank God for that. Now, before we get going, let's see if we can't propel a little soup out of those old bowels of yours before it's too late. Perhaps a first gasper just to be certain of a result. Where on earth have those Vestas got to? Don't want to have to push too hard, that's the thing. Go easy on those piles Blue, otherwise we'll have a blood bath on our hands. Hah, the governor's lighter, that'll do. Curious the effect they have—just the thought of a Dunhill's enough to open the floodgates. *Whooosh!* Now, quick over to the closet Blue, stop pissing about. That's an order.

There, that's better. What now? Ought to open that sodding door again, I suppose. Christ Blue, there's already a couple hanging about in the street! Quick, before they start beating on the windows, planting their greasy paws all over the shop front.

Good day, sir. Good day to you, young lady. How can I be of assistance? Very well. Just browsing, sir? Feel free. Don't let Blue get in your way! Now, first things first Blue, need to get your priorities right. Let's get that kettle on to begin with, then another gasper. Then perhaps we can see what tasks need doing. Who knows, with any luck extra troops will have arrived by then. Good job you're in charge, that's all I can say Blue.

Huh, speak of the devil! Good day Teeny. Julian. Er, could I just have a quick word Julian? Yes, well, there's a very pressing task which needs urgent attention with which I think your capable hands perhaps would care to be entrusted—get that kettle on would you, Julian? Oh, you're nipping round to the café are you? Well, let's see, er . . . in that case I'll have a tea and a bacon butty if you'd be so kind. Yes, sir, how can I be of assistance? Bolivia? Try the travel section, sir, downstairs on the left. Not at all. Now, where did I put that list? Here we are. Let's have a look then.

HOOVER
CLASSICS
DELIVERY (PENTANGLE BOOKS)
SHIFT G&L
VERA STERNE
PO
WINDOW DISPLAY
AOB

Huh. Got your work cut out for you there Blue. Better get going, stop pissing about! Jesus, and it's ten o'clock already! This will never do. On Blue, get your battle plan in order. Let's see. Hoovering. Shouldn't take long, say half an hour at the outside: say ten to ten-thirty. That's about right. Then tackle the Classics section: ten-thirty to eleven-thirty, say. That should do it. That'll still leave an hour or so to quash a few other jobs before lunch—with any luck the delivery should turn up around twelve, though God knows, it could arrive next week—then take a break around one. Just leave it there Julian. Obliged indeed. Don't forget to ring Vera Sterne in the lunch hour either. Vera Sterne—I don't suppose that's her real appellation. Just check your booking for tonight. Right, let's get cracking! Er, Julian, while you're breakfasting you wouldn't oblige by holding the fort for a few seconds would you, I just need to give the carpet the once over. Yes, very true, Julian. Now, let's see if we can't get this place in order for once before the governor gets here, he'll be giving us our redundancy notice if we don't.

Heavens above! Where the governor procured this fiasco of a hoover with its grinning cat's face God alone knows. I suppose he got it on the cheap, as per usual—no doubt it'll break down like all the other hoovers we've had here over the years. Sooner the better, in Blue's opinion. Sooner the better. It looks ridiculous, especially with that great black tube poking out of it where the nose should be, like that creature in *Galactic Wars*. Could give one of the clients a nasty turn! An elephant would have been *slightly* less incongruous. Not that I'd be *keen* even then, to be sure. I suppose the idea is to put a bit of fun into hoovering. Pah! That'll be the day. Certainly doesn't present the right front for a serious bookshop in Blue's opinion. You wouldn't find the likes of it in Waterstone's, that's for sure.

Strewth, I'd forgotten those boxes were still there. Just have to hoover round the things for now, though we'd better try and shift the lot later on. Could do with getting rid of all that crap on the lower shelves too, sitting there gathering dust. Where does all this blessed dust originate, that's what I'd like to know. Beg your pardon, sir. Of course, a lot of it enters the shop with the books, particularly the second hand ones, a lot of which have been sitting around in attics for donkey's years. But that doesn't explain *all* of it, not for a second it doesn't. You can believe Blue, the dust in here is *unnatural*. Teeny was saying only the other day that we ought to be issued with breathing apparatuses, or else have a whip round and get these ourselves. And in the stock area it's even worse—down there on a bad day it's a regular pea-souper.

Well, it hasn't had the dazzling effect you hoped for, but that'll have to do for now. What do you think, Julian? Yes, very true. Obliged, Julian. Now, what about a bite of that butty Blue? You'll need it to get you through till lunch, that's for sure. Sorry, sir. I'll be with you in a second. No respite for the wicked Blue. Buying or selling, sir? If you'd just like to bring it round here, sir, I'll see what I can do for you. Now, what have we here? Forster, Coover, Ishiguro, O'Neill, Blythe. Spanking new or not, we can't give you a lot for hardback fiction, sir, I should tell you that now. Sade, Bataille, *The Story of O.* Hnnn, interesting edition. Ronald Duncan. Would that be the librettist, sir? Yes, I think you could say that. *Gliding for Beginners, A Juggler's ABC.* Not a great future in those. *The Beats.* Could we say £15-00 for the lot, sir? Right you are. Obliged, indeed.

Now, don't beat about the bush Blue, you'd better tackle that Classics section before another job crops up. On your knees old boy, don't want to cripple your back, today of all days. Vera Sterne would be very upset. Now, let's see if we can introduce a little order here, whip out the worst of the bunch and arrange the rest alphabetically. Waterfall, P.J., *Drainage Slopes: Design & Function.* Well, that can go for a start. Should never have been allowed here in the first place. God above, there really is a lot of rubbish down here Blue. Half of these could go straight in the bin. Addison—hah!—who was asking for that the other day? No wonder I couldn't find it down here with the Rs. Heavens, there goes the blower again. Teeny! Where's she got to now? Teeny! Sod it, better take it yourself Blue. Hello, Bruised Books Ltd, how can I be of assistance? No, terribly sorry, I think you have the wrong connection. Not at all.

Oooerrrgh! This is backbreaking work, you can rest assured—squatting down here scraping around the Classics section just about takes the biscuit. I keep telling the governor to junk the lot. And why he's reluctant I haven't the foggiest. It's not as if anyone actually buys any of it. In fact the clients don't even *see* this lot tucked away as they are down here on the lower shelves. It's really beyond belief. He doesn't realise that nobody wants to read Cowper these days, let alone Lever, Clever, Waterfall, Dryden and the rest of the bunch. And who's to point the finger? Even the scholars aren't interested, they want the annotated editions, usually the Longley series, and we don't get a lot of those. Even when we do they go straight in the window and are snapped up in seconds.

Oooghherrnondy!

It's all right everyone! Just Blue's back playing up again! Definitely your FINAL WARNING Blue, no two ways about it. Take it easy old boy, don't want to overdo it.

Have a gasper.

And why not treat yourself to a Batchelors' cup-a-soup as well Blue, while you're at it, there's an idea. First get that kettle on though. Julian, could I trouble you for a second—I think we ought really to get that kettle on. A bit of a breather before the governor gets here, or we won't know what's hit us. You know what he's like. Now, how are we doing? Twelve-thirty. Already! Doesn't look like Pentangle are going to turn up before lunch. Best thing you can do is take a quick break Blue. Then lunch at one o'clock sharp. Don't forget to ring Vera Sterne either.

Wonder if she'll wear those long riding boots again tonight? Sorry, sir, did you speak? Poetry? Through the door on your right, sir. Foreign poetry downstairs. Not at all. Spurs last week. Wonder if she'll have that gear on again tonight? Yes, I'll have a cup-a-soup if you please Julian. Chicken and celery, if there's any left. Now, better light that gasper Blue, can't be standing here all day.

Hello, don't say the blessed CCTV's on the blink again. Perhaps just not focussed properly. Let's have a quick look, now. Hnnnnn. Is that any . . . no. Not a lot Blue, not a lot. Not that you can see a great deal even at best. You can just about pick out a person's shape on those rare occasions when one chances to venture downstairs, but even then visibility's so poor it's difficult to see what they're up to. Perhaps it works as a deterrent, though. Just leave it on the counter, Julian. I suppose that's the idea in any case, though you'd need to be pretty desperate to pinch anything out of our geography section. Good luck to the needy's what I say. Thank you, sir. Is there a student card with that? A student card. Yes, we offer 10% discount. No? That's £7-50 then, thankyou. Very obliged. Ahh, that's better. Should be able to follow it up with a solid lunch shortly, go to that place round the corner which does the all-day breakfast. Sausage, chips, egg and beans for £2-00. That should set you up again Blue. Wonder where the governor's got to? Probably suffering the gout again I shouldn't wonder. Says it's hereditary. Too frequent late nights and bubbly breakfasts if you ask Blue. Not that anyone does.

Nearly there. Just ten then off to lunch Blue. You can do it. Sorry, Julian? Well, there's plenty of pricing to do. You could start with the new fiction. As you like. Yes, two o'clock would be fine. Perhaps you'd hold fort again while Blue's at lunch. Very good.

Five to one. Get your coat Blue. Yes, sir. Downstairs, that's right. Now, those Vestas. Where on earth are they? Huh. Don't worry, the governor isn't going to notice his lighter just the once. See you shortly, Julian. Help yourself to a cup-a-soup if you feel so inclined. Yes, I take your point.

Afternoon, governor. Lighter? No, I don't believe I have. Oh, Pentangle phoned did they? Soon? Fair do. They're still downstairs, unless Julian's been at work on that front. No, fairly quiet on the whole. Right you are.

What's that Teeny? Just a second. Ah, good day to you, sir. Goods for Bruised Books Ltd, yes, that's us. You'll be wanting a hand unloading, I suppose. I'll just gather the troops, we weren't sure when to expect you. I see. Julian! Julian! Grab the trolleys would you, Julian, we're ready to unload.

Typical of the governor not to lift a finger. Always leaves Blue in charge when there's drudgery to be done. Just pass those down here, sir, that should do it. Christ, they're heavy enough. Watch your back Blue, bend at the knee. That's the way. Careful how you go, Teeny, we don't want any wounded. Huh! Try telling that to the governor! Now, where should we stack these, I wonder? Eventually, we'll want the lot downstairs for sorting and pricing, but we'd better just have a pile to begin with. Have to be in the back of the shop, I suppose, though it wouldn't worry Blue stacking the lot in front of G&L I can tell you. Not sure the governor would be bothered either, though it could upset Julian. It was his brainchild, after all—though why the governor gave Julian the go ahead heaven only knows. Probably thought it would sell well. Pah! Just there in the corner, that's the way Teeny. It's not a serious worry, but I'd prefer subjects like G&L to be located downstairs, out of the way, rather than out in the open. Just one on here, sir. How are we doing? Very good. I'll tell Julian to bring out another trolley. Where do I sign? Not at all. Very obliged.

Phew! Well that's that. Now, while there's a lull with the others off on their lunch break, you'd better just check that list of yours Blue, see what needs doing. Where are we now?

~~HOOVER~~
~~CLASSICS~~
~~DELIVERY (PENTANGLE BOOKS)~~
SHIFT G&L
~~VERA STERNE~~
PO
WINDOW DISPLAY
AOB

Half way there Blue, half way there. Perhaps tackle G&L now, seeing Julian's out, should get that over before he's back. Then the PO and finish off with the display if you can. But be sure you're away by five though, or you'll not catch the five twenty-five express. Vera Sterne's expecting you Blue, don't want to let her down! Said she was looking forward to it too, that saucy tone in her voice again. On Blue, get those books shifted, that's the way. You can do it. Christ, better go careful—sorry, sir!—on those stairs, they're steep enough *without* a load. That's the way. We'll get those on the shelf in just a second. Now, back for another load Blue. *Poof!* At least the exercise should do you good Blue. Don't get enough of it these days. Didn't get enough of it in *those* days! Perhaps ate just a bit too big a lunch old boy—let's hope you can still fit into Vera's cuirass. Crikey, watch your step Blue. Needs seeing to really that loose carpet. Strange idea, dressing your clients up like that, but I've no objections. Certainly, there's a sensuality about steel next to your skin. Hides the flab too. I wonder where she picked up the idea? Oh, I beg your pardon sir! Perhaps it's just Blue she does it for, who knows? Her little cuirassier. Says he has a warlike bearing.

There, that should do it. Now get the sods on the shelves Blue, that's the way. Needn't worry about alphabetical order, just get the things out of the way, that's what counts. *Prrrrrph!* I do beg your pardon. It's not right, in Blue's opinion, and that's all there is to it. Personally, I accuse the schooling. Laxity, lack of discipline—that's at the root of it all, no doubt about it. There, that should do for now. Clears a bit of space upstairs at least.

There's the governor calling. What can he be after? Hold on, I'll be there in a jiffy! Easier said than done Blue, easier said than done. Yes? Pricing? Certainly. I'll get cracking straight away. Now, where's the Whittaker gone, I wonder? Last saw it over by Classics. Yes, there we are. Start with this box to begin with. Let's see what we have here. E.V. Fitts-Willis *Cybernetics and Cyberspace.* Can't see there's going to be a huge call for that, but at least it looks up to date. Not really your field is it Blue? Let's see now. Fitts-, Fitts-, Fitts-Waller, Fitts-Wellings, Fitts-Willis, E.V. £45-99. Huh. We're certainly not going to shift it at that price. Let's try £15-00. What's next? Bryan Knocker *Beyond Differentials: Calculus & Hypercalculus.* Worst part of the day this, and it's one of those tasks that's never really finished. As soon as you're through one load there's always another just arrived. Knitter, Knivett, Knobler, Knoblock, Knock, Knocker. It's not quite so killing when you know the field, of course, but even then the pleasure is attached to a certain pain, usually in the backside. R.D. Drake *Astrophysics Now.* Not Blue's cup of tea. Drab, Draffin, Drag, Dragon, Drain, Drakakis, Drake. Jesus, there are a lot of these. Drake P., Drake Q., Drake R.A., Drake R.C., Drake R.D. Here we are. £17-99. Try £8-00. Not as bad as Jones of course, but quite a few nonetheless. Wonder if he's a descendent of Sir Francis? He got around a bit by all accounts. Wouldn't be allowed today. Not even royalty can get away with it. Bartlebooth. Shouldn't be a lot of those. As I thought. Hole in one.

On Blue, you can do it. Keep your head down old boy, it's the only way, like digging trenches. Deardon. That's an odd one. Like the start of a letter. Got it. Ah, Fitts-Willis again, what did we put that one at? £15-00, yes. That's the best thing about these bulk deliveries, several copies of the one book if you're lucky. Brickbatt. About all that can be said in their favour if you'll allow Blue to say so.

That's enough of that for now. Besides, if you don't shift soon Blue, the PO will be shut. Ah! Better check the governor doesn't want anything sending special delivery.

Er, could I trouble you on the subject of the afternoon post? Yes, I see. That's all in order, I believe. And are there any packages for the special delivery service this afternoon? No? Fine. Well Blue, just those two parcels downstairs for Zurich then. In which case it can *wait*. I'll pop those in on the way to the station, save the extra journey. Ah, Julian. I . . . er . . . felt it . . . *better off* there if you understand. Yes. I don't deny it. Very true. Yes. A cup of tea would be splendid. Two sugars if you please, I'll hold fort. Just one second, young lady. Thankyou. Is there a student card with that? That'll be £6-00 then please. Obliged. Quick, better put the governor's lighter back now the coast's clear. There. What now? Jesus, the blower again. On Blue, you can do it. Hello, Bruised Books Ltd, how can I be of assistance, sir? Yes, we do stock a wide range of historical texts, sir. Any particular publication? I see. No, I don't think we have a copy of that available at this instant, but you're entitled to browse, our stock changes on a daily basis. Yes, thank you for calling, sir.

Ah, Julian, I'd nearly forgotten. Just pop it on the counter would you? Obliged, indeed. Now, what are we now, I wonder? Huh, three-thirty already. Flies when you're enjoying yourself! Oh bugger, looks like the teabag's broken again. Another of the governor's false savings: the only teabags in the world which need a tea-strainer. Now, where are those biscuits Blue? There we are. And the scissors, they were here a second ago, I could have sworn. Where on earth have they got to? You'll have to sort this out Blue. Christ! It's no wonder you can never find anything in this place the state it's in. Lord knows, Blue's always eager to create a little order, but you're fighting a losing battle in this place, I can assure you. Teeth Blue, use your teeth and let there be an end of it. There, that should do it. Just one second, sir. No rest for the wicked Blue. Buying or selling? If you'd like to bring yourself round here, sir, I'll see what I can do. Right, what have we here now? Huh, *Buddha: An Introduction,* Augustine *City of God.* An interesting book, sir. Yes. *Icons in Renaissance Art, The Flagellation of Christ.* A nice little collection, sir. We haven't any call for the Buddha, here, but I'll give you £20-00 for the rest, you can't say fairer than that. Very obliged. Not at all.

Get that tea down you Blue, that's the way. Put you back on the straight and narrow. *Prrrrpp!* Real gut rot that lunch has left you with, probably all that greasy food again Blue. You don't learn, do you? Can't keep off it. Now, before it's too late Blue, I'd get cracking on that window display. Looks like a hurricane's hit it right now.

Let's see now, just the once over with the duster for starters, don't piss about Blue. Christ, there's plenty of dust here too. Though I don't think anyone's been round here with a duster for ages. *Achoooooghh!* Jesus! How's that whip round for the breathing apparatuses going then Teeny? I could certainly do with one over here! Right, a prize piece to fill the place of those tatty leather bound things that have been squatting over there for the last few weeks. Yes, why not Augustine, nothing beats a pious facade. What else? Could try a row of those new Pentagon books, that's the way. Here we are. Lord, is that still there? Huh! No wonder at that price! One of the governor's bright ideas. Put it at £6-50 Blue, that should do it. Now, finish off with a few art books just to brighten things up a bit. Pissarro, just the ticket. Teeny, I don't suppose I could trouble you just to nip outside and tell Blue how the window looks? Obliged. Gauguin, he'll do. Well? Looks all right does it Teeny? Right-ho! Obliged indeed.

Where are we now, then? Four-thirty. Huh, better not piss about Blue, still got the PO on the way to the station, then an evening to savour with any luck! Nobody can say you haven't earned it either Blue. Christ no! The unsurpassable Vera Sterne will no doubt be taking your cuirass off the wall this very second Blue, giving it an affectionate little polish with her blouse, slipping into her boots and spurs, unfurling her whip. . . . Sir! I beg your pardon. Not at all. Is there a student card with that, sir? Yes, we offer a 10% discount. Very good. £10-00 to you sir. Obliged.

Now, before there's a to-do, you'd better get your skates on Blue, I think that post needs urgent attention. And you'd better stop for a bit of cash too, we wouldn't want Vera to be dissappointed in you. That would never do. She'd punish you severely if you pulled that one on her Blue, rest assured! She'd posteriorise you good and proper. Without a shadow of a doubt. Better just tell the governor, so he can hold fort.

Yes. First class. Rest assured. Until Friday, then. Teeny. Julian. Don't forget your gaspers Blue. Sorry, what did you say? Yes, I take your point.

DREG

IN

He took the job out of necessity, nothing better being on offer, needing the work, the money. He'd seen it outlined on one of the Job Centre posters, red on white. He'd ignored it to begin with, instinctively dismissed it even, yet by the end of the week when he'd unsuccessfully tried the other possible outlets (*The Inquirer*, the post office, the corner shop window), he thought why not? Everybody needed to begin somewhere. Besides, he'd nothing to lose.

TOPS

Receiving the forms by return of post, he proceeded to fill them in directly, beginning with his country of origin, then on to his employment history—of which precious little—finishing up with his hobbies. He'd little to write here too, not being one to indulge himself in chess or judo, or even outdoor sports, for on the whole he disliked clubs, but in the end he put down swimming, then tennis, though he didn't swim often, nor frequent the tennis courts. The form in the post, he went into the closest sports shop, emerging with two white tops.

OPT

Deep down he'd not expected to get invited for interview. He'd only two previous ones under his belt, both of which ended up with him being weeded out before the second set. He'd been dismissed with words of succour both times, counsel on improving his CV, his exposition, his dress sense, which he'd interpreted, correctly, to imply don't phone us we'll phone you. So when the letter turned up on his doorstep informing him of the time of the interview he felt mildly stunned. Yet he turned up in good time, spoke on cue, nodded on cue, even smiled on cue, then, to his surprise, got offered the job. He even thought of refusing it to begin with, thinking to himself he'd never been entirely serious—for who'd opt to collect rubbish for their living?—then the money could definitely be more inciting, but in the end, for better or worse, he took it: Disposer of Refuse & Ecologic Goods (support level).

IN

One uniform, blue.
Two boots, brown.
One oilskin, yellow (fluorescent).
One torch.
One set nose-clips, brown rubber.

IMMOBILE

During his one month test period time went quickly. He got up before five for his eight hour shift, which left him tired in the extreme, immobile, then spent his free time in bed. But nevertheless he felt things were going well. Besides, if they weren't, deep down, he didn't mind. In working he fulfilled his role for society, kept the work ethic lobby content—here he'd include his mother—but if he didn't come through the test period with flying colours, deep down, he didn't mind. He'd been content to just cruise, job or no job, so if he ended up on the dole once more, his month up, so be it. He'd no problem himself living like he'd been until recently, unemployed, immobile, prospectless, bored.

SMELL

There were some surprises in store for him, foremost of which the smell. None of his fellow workmen, he noticed, used the issued nose-clips, looking on them indeed with contempt. They preferred their own methods. Some smoked pungent roll-ups, Old Holborn or Drum, which hung from their lips like fuses. Others crunched strong mints, which they were forever offering round. Others still simply inspired through the mouth, finding they got used to it once through the first few bins. In short, the nose-clips were no-noes. Still, curiously, he found he liked the smell.

OUT

One set nose-clips, brown rubber.

RUGS

While the weeks went by, quickly bringing him into his second month without upset—the test period, it turned out, mere custom— he discovered the city, including districts he'd not known to exist (green belt neighbourhoods with imposing mock Tudor buildings served by long drives, modern housing developments cutting into the surrounding countryside) with the method of one inspecting new rugs from the wrong side. He found he could guess the prosperity of different neighbourhoods from the constitution of their refuse. The poorer districts would disgorge endless tins of dogfood, boxes of Kellog's Frosties, ketchup bottles; while in the refuse of the richer districts one found broken hickory pipes, empty wine bottles, even every so often the odd item which his fellows were quick to procure for themselves: stereos in good working order, television sets, cotton shirts.

DUST

One week with his fellow workmen he'd to empty the contents of the house of the retired London eye doctor, Mortimer French. The moment he stepped into the building he found himself overcome by the powerful smell of extinction; here, like with the smell of the more routine refuse, he found he enjoyed it. While they threw up clouds of dust, quickly settled since the doctor's recent demise, piling up stools, oculist eye testers, lenses, old books, in surroundings of mounting sobriety, he felt the oddest sense of homecoming, the scene flooding his mind with memories of his uncle Len whose house he remembered being emptied in just this style. Then he understood this smell which he found himself so bewitched by to be the smell of the dying.

IN

One monocle, with silver rim (lens missing).
One box Pickwick nibs.
One eye (perspex).
One Peugeot coffee grinder (rim split).
Two pipes.

CERBERUS

The quilt of fog which descended on the city the next morning distorted well-known contours beyond recognition. Bins suddenly turned into hellish monsters looming up from the murk, doors into terrifying torture devices from which no egress. Numerous times the truck took wrong turnings owing to the poor visibility. Even his torch proved of little service. The only things which persisted unmodified were the repetitive noises of the truck's twin grinder while, like some huge two-mouthed Cerberus, it relentlessly devoured the rubbish they fed it.

DISCONCERTED

One lunchtime in the refectory, he found himself sitting opposite some new recruits from Revenue. If rumour were to be trusted, they'd been hired to improve efficiency—in other words, to trim the workforce. Listening in on their colloquy, it disconcerted him to find himself one of the DREGS, the monicker derived from the infelici- tously worded title of his specific division of the refuse collecting set: Disposer of Refuse & Ecologic Goods. The ecologic goods re- ferred to the council's development scheme no. 471 whereby house- holds were supplied with free bin-liners into which they were to put refuse for recycling. The DREGS were the lowest level workers in the firm. Common household rubbish—unfinished foodstuffs, old clothes, used boxes—fell to them.

SPEC

The next week, on spec, he went to the interment of Mortimer French in the cemetery over the river. There were few present, be- sides the personnel—French, it seemed, outlived most of his friends—so there were plenty of empty pews in the gloomy meeting house. The obsequies over, there followed the brief procession then the lowering of the coffin into its pit, presided over by the priest, with the help of the interment director who supervised his busy per- sonnel. Like these shuffling men in their sombre clothes, it sud- denly struck him, he'd become involved in the city's unseen under- world. These men were his brothers: while they presided over rites of interment, removing corpses so the living could get on with their business unimpeded, he presided over the beyond of junk—used newsprint, spilt food, old clothes—which likewise needed removing so the world could continue in its routine. Like them, he'd become one of the city's unseen ministers of extinction.

BIN-LINERS

From time to time, over mugs of coffee, his fellow workers would swop stories from former times. None of them were old enough to remember the horse-pulled rubbish vehicles of the twenties, but most remembered well the hefty unlined zinc bins they once shoul- dered for their living, pellets of food stuck like limpets to their in- sides. Most, too, were in concurrence over the single step which most revolutionised the job, the introduction of the modern bin- liner, enclosing the detritus in its smooth flexible skin, helping col- lection no end, while rendering the whole exercise less offensive. Its only inconvenience, serious enough without doubt, could be put succinctly: it rendered the jettisoned goods invisible, so worthwhile items were thus more difficult to find. Yet by the weight, the feel of the bin-liner, one could often guess the contents, even if close inspection proved dicey. Frequently, though, one threw into the grinder bin-liners which seemed full of soggy kitchen refuse, only to see their spilt contents disclose some fine woollen jumpers. Then one could open bin-liners sure they would be stuffed with electric goods, only to find them full of empty tins of rice pudding. Yet in this business persistence could bring rich returns.

IN

One chess set (white rook missing).
One tie.
One pottery bird.
One copy *Spurt*.

PROPENSITY

Coming up to the end of his second month, settling well into the routine of work, even to the extent of building up some kind of bond with his fellows—one of them he'd even met outside working hours for snooker—he understood for the first time the secret necessity which, from the beginning, drove him unwittingly to find his current employment. In other words, he understood how, curiously, his finishing up collecting refuse couldn't, in the end, be considered the fluke of contingency he'd thought it. For better or worse, his job fulfilled one of the secret propensities of his being—in short his perverse interest in extinction, the defunct, dissolution, demise, ruin. He felt it strongly in the house of Mortimer French, then once more during the service, then he felt it every morning too, confronted with the smell of the bins.

BOXES

In his childhood, he remembered, he'd found it thrilling to rip the legs off insects, storing their dismembered bodies in little boxes. He'd enjoyed too holding the spirit in his lungs till his body rocked on the edge of sensibility.

PUNCTURED

One morning spent in the seedier side of the city— the district being more often covered by other trucks—turned out to be full of surprises. The district, one of the city's most extensive, proved unexpectedly quick to service, for in lieu of the routine six or seven bin-liners per household there were on the whole only one or two. Then while the refuse of most neighbourhoods consisted chiefly of used food boxes, here there were none, which left one wondering if the people round here ever fed properly. The refuse in this district consisted mostly of binned news, household objects—from pictures to items of furniture—suggesting nobody stopped here long. Other refuse included: one rubber doll (punctured); three brightly coloured rubber rings; one bicycle pump.

IN

One egg timer.
One bicycle pump.

SUSPENDED

He spent the evening in, browsing through the copy of *Spurt* he'd recently found. It proved on the whole undistinctive of its genre, except possibly in one extended photo-sequence depicting three zombielike women in some kind of dungeon or crypt, from the ceiling of which hung two girls, seemingly unconscious, in their wedding dresses. Of those on offer he found this sequence the most enticing. The women, dressed in stockings with high heels, crowned in blonde wigs, set upon their consorts' bodies with tongues, fingers, mouths, even toes, until, in the concluding shot, they slumped motionless on the floor, under the suspended brides, mouths open in synthetic bliss. With his eyes devouring this picture, his fingers twined round his surprise, he pulled himself to the edge of oblivion.

SPIGOT

The next morning he woke well beyond his given time, missing the truck setting off, so took the bus in order to rejoin his fellows, who'd by this point completed most of the round. They greeted him with condescension—it seemed he'd broken one of the revered rules of refuse collecting—then, hoping to redeem himself, he pulled his weight twice over, but still the others were cold, unresponsive. There'd been fresh rumour of Revenue thinning down the workforce, one of them pointed out. If this proved true, he thought, he'd be the first to go. The evening he spent on his own, in his bedsit, losing himself in the repetitive criss-crossing design on his ceiling, listening to the spigot dripping in the kitchen, too tired to get up to fix it.

IN

One model glider, wooden (wing missing).

LIMBO

From time to time, finding himself with little else to do, he would distribute over his floor the objects he'd procured during his period of employment, now entering its third month. The objects which most bewitched him, he found, were curiously not those which were the most useful, like the boots or the tie, but those whose usefulness tended to zero, the monocle (lens missing), the coffee grinder (rim split), the chess set (white rook missing), the glider (wing missing). His interest in these objects could be connected with their very impoverishment, which rendered them suspended in limbo, neither being the things they seemed, nor not being those things. Strictly, the words for these objects did not yet exist. He would occupy himself, sometimes for hours on end, inventing neologisms for these incongruous objects. Why did the world ignore them, fostering this groundless division between things, useful or not? Denied their rights by the world in its self-seeking pursuit of utility, these curious objects were for him touchstones which signified his crossing of forbidden borders, bore witness to his love with their kiss of extinction.

TURFED

One night he woke from disturbing unconscious stimuli. He'd pictured himself climbing into one of his household bin-liners from which, subsequently, he'd found egress impossible. He'd then lost consciousness. Once more in possession thereof he'd noticed the churning sound, then felt the pelvic jolt when turfed into the grinder. Its noise drowned out his thoughts. He cried out. Woke.

OILSKIN

The following morning they covered the routine streets, collecting the routine refuse in their routine order. Due to the light drizzle it proved sensible to don the yellow oilskin, which while it protected one from the elements, grew sticky-hot on the inside. To liven up the morning he doggedly explored the contents of numerous bin-liners, but none held much of distinction.

IN

One sieve (rusting).

EMERGENCY

One weekend, finding himself on his own—he never phoned his friends now, nor they him—he inventoried the objects he'd found, listing the words he'd coined for those without. He couldn't decide whether or not the sieve required one, for while unbroken—its only holes being those it required to function—its rusty condition rendered it dodgy. In the end he christened it his EMERGENCY SIEVE. The rest of the weekend he spent home, eyeing his distorted reflection in the dirty windows. Brooding on the word which now signified his own self, he wrote it with his finger in the dust: DREG.

CUT

The end of the weekend he spent browsing once more through his copy of *Spurt,* once more finding himself seduced by the photo-sequence depicting three zombielike women in some kind of dungeon or crypt, from the ceiling of which hung two girls, seemingly unconscious, in their wedding dresses. The women, dressed in stockings with high heels, crowned in blonde wigs, set upon their consorts' bodies with tongues, fingers, mouths, even toes, until, in the concluding shot, they slumped motionless on the floor, under the suspended brides, mouths open in synthetic bliss. He found the sequence beginning to excite him, like it did before, but this time he found his excitement punctured by the sudden perception of the women's joyless eyes, which looked without exception in his direction. The sequence did not, then, find its centre in the women's own desires, but in those of its expected viewer. Moreover, it courted this viewer not only with the women in the foreground, but with the suspended brides. In other words, it courted him with the lure of two brides who were *not conscious,* possibly *not even living.* This thought sufficed to fill him with horror, of his own desire. With scissors, he cut the *Spurt* into numberless thin strips, depositing them in the bin.

OUT

One copy *Spurt* (stripped).

NOSE-CLIPS

During his fourth month on the job the summer broke in its full force, the uncollected bin-liners grilling in the morning sun. Even tied, the smell could be so powerful he found himself for the first time regretting the nose-clips. The detritus inside the bins, moreover, seemed to swell under the sun's influence, while the skin of the bin-liner wilted, which rendered the rotting contents likely to spill out onto the ground. When they did you were supposed to scoop up the mess, but didn't.

JUGGLER

Coming home by the city centre he stopped on seeing some young boys juggling in the precinct. The best juggled three clubs, one of which, from time to time, he guided under his leg without letting it drop. Every so often, too, he would project one of the clubs into the sky, twenty feet or more, while continuing to toss the other two, then would effortlessly reintroduce it into the round on its descent. The boy possessed enormous skill, but his connection with these clubs could only be described in terms of love. No other sight he'd ever seen seemed so full of joyful possibility, triumph, overcoming; yet he left the scene filled not only with hope, but sorrow too.

NOTICE

The next morning in work he got summoned to report directly to the boss's office. When he got there reception told him to hold on for ten minutes. Fifteen went by before they told him to go in. The boss told him to sit down, so he did, then the girl from Revenue spelled out the position. If they were to continue to be effective under competitive conditions it would be requisite to introduce efficiency cuts in the workforce. The budget for the next revenue period would be down by 32 percent beginning next month. Under these conditions—he felt it coming—his recent employment on support level couldn't be defended. Hindmost in, frontmost out. They regretted the short notice, but hoped he'd comprehend their position: they'd been fighting up until the very end to prevent these cuts. Did he get the picture?

ON

Seconds on he found himself stood in the corridor once more, still chewing over the news. To begin with he felt shocked by the pronouncement, for in his four months he'd done his work with diligence. He took his work seriously—he'd even believed sometimes he'd found his profession. But then who knows, he thought. Possibly the opportunity to move on—forcibly or not—should be seized. Even the dole he could cope with, even grow to like once more—he felt sure of it—yet now he'd got one job under his belt why shouldn't he set his sights higher? He felt the pull of obscure futures tug his body, fill his being with sudden unexpected energy. Briefly, it felt like he surveyed the city—its life, its options, soft or otherwise—from some high-up point, like the top of some hill, or high-rise building, though in truth he did no such thing. He turned, pursed his lips, took himself off.

OUT

Bin-liners, grinders, dust, nose-clips, spilt food, the odd find: he'd felt their secret powers of seduction, to be sure, sometimes with such power he might've worshipped them. But in the end, despite this hidden promise, such things were poor friends. This only proved it. He took off his uniform, his boots, slipped into his leisure clothes then out, into the street. He'd spent too much time under the blind spell of this grimy underworld, he thought. Four months too much.

MONITOR

There are thirty-six cameras in the store which are all linked to the central monitoring office where I sit from nine till five-thirty five days a week and from nine till six on Saturday.

SCRN7 LWRGRND CM006 13.03

A man in his mid-thirties wearing a blue anorak, jeans and trainers, leans over the freezer and takes out a box of frozen cod fillets in herb sauce. He reads the nutritional information deliberately then, having satisfied his curiosity, tosses it into his wire basket. He walks slowly in the direction of the bread and delicatessen, then jerks suddenly to a standstill, his eye caught by a rack of sandwiches in their see-through boxes and an assortment of variously embalmed ready-to-eat meat offerings.

The cameras are distributed unevenly over the store's three floors. There are six on food and kitchenware (low-risk), eighteen on ladies' clothes (high-risk), and twelve on menswear and footwear (medium-risk).

SCRN2 FRST CM027 13.06

A man in overalls stands examining ties, a large green holdall, unclosed, at his feet.

This sounds like quite a lot, but given an average turnover of four thousand customers a day—and on Saturday it far exceeds this—there's a lot of room for error. Having only six cameras on food and kitchenware leaves a lot of hidden corners, the most serious of which is doubtless dairy where action moves offscreen round about the cream buns.

SCRN7 LWRGRND CM001 13.08

A customer in black leggings cranes forward over the fridge unit to reach a slice of cheesecake which she lowers into her wire basket. Behind her there is the image of a dark-haired girl with closed eyes taking into her mouth a sizeable choux bun. The carefully manicured fingernails of her chocolate-covered hands, coloured bright red, contrast calculatedly with the thick white cream which oozes from the bun's end.

Items such as sieves, coffee grinders and kitchen scissors are rarely taken so they are shelved together and remain unmonitored. The unmonitored areas are low risk but our store detectives do their best to cover them nonetheless. The cameras on the whole tend to be situated so as to cover high-risk sites: silk shirts, lingerie, wine and liqueurs. Thieves who know what they're doing tend to go for goods with a high-cost value. So long as they're easy to move on the streets. To be sure, we lose the odd bag of sweets or fig roll, but this is nothing to get alarmed about.

SCRN2 FRST CM027 13.10

The man in overalls walks away from ties, taking his holdall with him. At least it's not a bomb. From the way it sags it must be only half-full. He walks in the direction of knitwear.

The store's thirty-six cameras are relayed to a total of nine screens in the monitoring room, stacked in a bank, three by three, on the wall. This means that only a quarter of the available information can be scanned at any one time, so the monitor has to be extremely vigilant, constantly juggling the images on the screens. It does no harm to know what you're looking for in advance, how to identify the likely candidate. Most thieves, before they make a snatch, tend to look around to check that the coast is clear, so if you see someone glancing from side to side you need to be on your toes.

SCRN6 FRST CM030 13.12

A young middle-aged man in jeans, naked from the waist, holds in his right hand an orange T-shirt which he is trying out for size. His wife, wearing a see-through chiffon blouse, stands at his side, looking on.

Another thing to look out for is a man and a woman working in a team, above all if they're with a baby. They often use the baby as a screen, both to give themselves an innocent family look and, if the baby is in a buggy, it's here that they stash the goods. I've seen men take hold of a whole rack of shirts at once, nine or ten items, and hang them on the back of a buggy while the woman shields them and then covers the lot with her coat.

SCRN5 GRND CM019 13.14

A smartly dressed woman in her thirties examines a new range of black lace underwear on show in lingerie. To test the softness of the material she holds it to her cheek, her mouth unclosing slightly as she does so to reveal a set of immaculate white teeth. Her dark hair is tightly curled and is held off her face by a silver hairband. Returning the item to its hanger she walks over to the other side of the stand, from where her full face is clearly visible. Her eyes are large and brown, like those of a doe. She looks around, uncomfortably, as if someone might be watching her.

Teenagers working in a gang is another thing to look out for—they tend to crowd the stand they're interested in, blocking it off from view before taking anything. Here of course it is very difficult to see the actual theft, but if you notice a gang acting in this way you can be sure nine times out of ten that's what they are about.

SCRN1 GRND CM007 13.17

In ladies' knitwear a fresh widow in a bright batik dress holds a small fluffy white dog under one arm while with the other she examines a red lambswool cardigan. As two elderly ladies brush by, the dog lets out a little bark which makes one of them start. She steadies herself on the arm of her friend. Over the shoulder of the fresh widow the image of a juvenile model wearing the same lambswool cardigan as on show is just discernible. She stands in a meadow beside a stone mill whose wheel is turned by an artificial waterfall. High above the meadow, in the background, floats a yellow glider.

Not everyone is cut out to make a good monitor. Like many jobs it requires individual skills. Some days are full of action and these can be quite exciting—you need to be constantly on the ball—but more difficult to tackle are those times when there is a lull. It's these moments which lead a lot of folk to think of monitoring as a dull and boring job, but it shouldn't be, not if you do it in the right frame of mind. I try to think of it as a kind of game. To win the game you would have to detect every single theft, see it coming in advance and alert the store detectives in good time so that no criminal ever got out of the store undetected. This is the dream, the bonanza, the jamboree.

SCRN4 FRST CM026 13.20

The man in overalls comes into sight once more, this time examining children's shoes. He is standing in front of a rack of brightly coloured trainers, one of which he holds in his hands as if testing it for weight. The large green holdall, unclosed, is still at his feet.

In the end, for intricate reasons to do with economics, this total victory is never attainable. The real battle, the target of the game, is therefore to maintain theft at an absolute minimum which may tend towards zero, but never quite reaches it. To do this you need to be constantly on the alert for the slightest sign of a likely candidate. The regular thieves are always on file and a fotofit image of them can be flashed on screen at the touch of a button. We're encouraged to commit their faces to memory, however, and I also try to read their whole files from time to time so as to get to know their characters. You might think that once somebody had been caught red-handed they would be inclined to take their business elsewhere, but not a bit of it. Many of these customers are obsessive thieves and even when they've been caught two or three times they'll come back for more. It's these obsessive ones who are the most variable, because they do it for the risk, the high. They are the real addicts of the scene, and nothing short of a stiff sentence is likely to deter them. Those who steal for the money tend to be clumsier on the whole, more nervous, since somewhere they still know that what they are doing is wrong.

SCRN4 GRND CM021 13.21

The smartly dressed woman, unclothed, stands before a full length mirror wearing an all-in-one bodice from the new range of black lace underwear on show in lingerie. Behind her a blind man hits the floor rythmically with his stick. The softness of the material is evidently to her liking. She stands erect with her shoulders back so that her chest is thrust forward. The outline of her breasts is clearly visible as she runs a finger down her back and onto the hem at the base of her buttocks.

Something to watch is the way customers behave around the changing rooms. The oldest trick in the book is for someone to go in with four items and come out with three and we have a disc system installed which tries to deal with this. But such a system is always at the risk of subterfuge so it is wise to maintain close surveillance at all times. For a long time security has argued for the installation of hidden cameras in the cubicles but management has on the whole been reluctant on legal grounds. This is a shame, because if some of the stories about what the customers get down to in there are true this would make very interesting viewing. One of the cleaners even found a condom in there last summer. Something else to watch for are customers tugging at the security tags. We have these attached to all high-cost value items of clothing and the girls at the tills remove them with a key once the customer has settled accounts, but often a strong sudden tug in the right direction is all it takes, though the garment may be damaged as a result.

SCRN9 GRND CM017 13.22

A woman in brown tights is standing by a selection of brightly coloured beach towels and swimming costumes. She has taken a small hand mirror out of her bag and holds it before her face as she adjusts her hair. To her left is a free-standing model, a beach ball under one arm, wearing a blue bikini and a smile of bliss. In front of the model, on the ground, two teenage girls, naked from the waist, roll a marble back and forth between them.

Nothing irregular about this woman most would think. But my training tells me that she might be making use of the mirror to check out the store: see where the security guards are at the moment, where the cameras are situated. Maybe I'll ask security to watch out for her.

SCRN8 LWRGRND CM002 13.23

An elderly woman with a blue rinse in a thick woollen coat is trying unsuccessfully to reach a box of biscuits on the highest shelf. She looks around for someone to aid her but she is alone in this corner of the store, at this hour. She stands still, staring at the box, accusingly.

It's very useful to maintain good relations with security on the whole. In the last analysis we work as a team and this should never be forgotten. Store detectives have a variety of functions. Not only are they the last barrier between the thief and the street but they can cover the hidden corners where the cameras can't go. If I have doubts about a certain customer who then moves offscreen the first thing I'll do is alert a store detective on the walkie-talkie. It's essential that a store detective should be able to maintain low visibility when necessary, however. If they're too obvious in the store then nobody ever steals anything.

SCRN6 GRND CM021 13.26

The smartly dressed woman stands before a full length mirror wear-

ing knickers and a bra from the new range of black lace underwear on show in lingerie. She holds her head back and observes her reflection in the mirror with an uncertain look. Stretching a hand over her left shoulder she unhooks the bra and lets it fall to the floor. She continues to gaze at herself in the mirror as if lost in reverie. With the bra removed her full breasts sag slightly under their own weight.

The trick is for the store detective to move away from a risk site just before the thief is going to strike. This serves to alleviate the thief's worries and to force them to make their move. This is a risky manoeuvre but usually works well so long as I have a clear view of them on camera. When we catch thieves they often seem astounded since they were sure the store detectives were out of sight—but this of course is just the intention. In thinking too much of the store detectives they forget about the cameras and then we have them caught. Teamwork.

SCRN2 LWRGRND CM005 13.30

A gentleman of the cloth carrying a bottle of wine in one hand and a box of ice-cream cones in the other stands in a checkout queue, mouth tightly closed, eyes raised heavenwards. In front of him a middle-aged woman wearing a scarlet jacket with gold buttons is buying a large box of assorted seafood nibbles, while her son tugs at her dress. He wears a black cotton T-shirt which reads: "Your story has truly moved me. It is not only truly sad but has the hallmark of real genuine loss and forbearance. Now before you say anything more **** off out of my way and let me be."

One of the things I most like about the job is the satisfaction of observing the women customers. It's not mentioned in my contract, of course, but it is one of those things which make the job worthwhile. And it makes amends for not having a girlfriend myself. I can choose from among the several hundred women in the store at any one time and I can look them over to my heart's content—after all, I'm only doing my job. Then if any of them takes my fancy, well, I can devote a little extra attention to her. Sometimes, I have to confess, above all with the flirty ones, I carry their image home in my head and then have my way with them over a hand job in the bath. I can't grumble really, with my own harem there for the taking. Every day brings something new.

SCRN8 LWRGRND CM003 13.32

An untidy man in a dark cylindrical greatcoat, buttoned to the neck, shuffles by the cheese counter. His shoes are just visible beneath the frayed hem of his greatcoat. They have been roughly daubed with white emulsion which obscures their original colour, and even their exact style. From a distance, with the addition of a bowler hat and a red nose, the man might be mistaken for a clown.

A regular customer this one. Always trying his chances on the wine and liqueurs. Very keen on cherry brandy according to his file. History of mental illness too, but with no traceable family he lives on the streets. A regular bum in a word. No matter how many times we catch him he always comes back for more. It's what we call the yo-yo effect in the trade: a kind of irresistible urge to return to the scene of the crime, act it out again.

SCRN9 GRND CM024 13.33

The woman in brown stockings is now entering the changing rooms. The girl in charge hands her a green disc (two items) but I am certain I can see something else, more brown tights maybe, tucked under her left arm, which she holds unnaturally close to her side. I should warn security.

It is frustrating not being able to see what she's doing in there. I might be letting a dead cert slide away from me. If we had cameras installed in the cubicles of course I'd be able to be more certain about the truth. As it stands she'll have a good chance of getting away with it. Or at worst get the benefit of the doubt. Even if I do maintain surveillance as she comes out. If she undresses and hides the brown tights in her knickers then nobody's going to be able to find them. Not even Max on security.

SCRN4 FRST CM029 13.34

The man in overalls is kneeling in front of a rack of green duffel coats, tying his shoelace. The unclosed green holdall is just visible at the base of the coats.

Even with increased security the number of thefts has hit a record high over the last year. How to tackle this rise is the most frequently discussed issue at our monthly security board meetings. A local constable from crime deterrence usually comes along and his recommendation is always the same: increase the number of cameras, monitors and security guards, and crime will fall.

SCRN4 FRST CM034 13.38

A child with a green woollen bonnet is tearing the magazine which sticks out of his father's jacket. The father is holding a cotton waistcoat out in front of him at arm's length.

But things never have been nor ever will be so straightforward. Above all, the economics of the situation have to be considered. The need for security in the first instance is of course financial. The firm can only sustain a certain amount of theft with comfort, and when this level is broken combative action needs to be taken: this is the birth of modern security. But security too—increasingly so today with the new technologies—costs money, so that a total security situation becomes untenable. In the end, a balance needs to be struck, between the loss of income incurred by theft and the costing of security, so as to maintain crime at a tolerable level. For better or worse, this is the reality of the situation, and this is why total victory can only remain a dream.

SCRN1 GRND CM008 13.40

An old woman with a blue rinse in a thick woollen overcoat is being escorted back into the store by two security guards. She is looking around for someone to come to her rescue but there is nobody available. One of the security guards carries a box of biscuits under his left arm.

Well I never. Mind you, I thought she was dangerous looking from the way she eyeballed that biscuit tin. But how did she get it down I wonder? It just shows you: nobody can be trusted these days, not even the elderly. And they're the first to grumble about the youth of today. I bet she'll blame her memory when she gets interrogated. That's a favourite trick with these older customers. Still, if she's a first offender they'll let her off with a warning and add her to the file. Just to shake her a bit. Teach her a lesson. Well, I guess this is one story she won't be telling her grandchildren in any case.

SESSION-MAN

The 60s and 70s are a blank. Your mind is a blank. There at least. A LAKE. That's what the doktr says. The doktr has a ginger beard and wavy dark hair, thinning on top but still strong & thik elsewhere. He is Welsh, though his aksnt is hard to detekt. When he smiles you kan see his gold krouns, at the bak. He is METIKulusLY Kleen, always in a hurry.

You have nothing against lakes. You like lakes. The only trouble is that this one's in your head.

The doktr asks you your birthday. You tell him. He asks you what size shoes you take. You say. He asks you your WAIST SIZE. You kan't remember, you say.

The nurse shines a tort shin your eyes. Then in your ears. Then up your nose. You hope she's not going to shine iT Up your aRse, you say. She doesn't.

Overnight someone pulls up all the motrwys. Ms 1-n. What happens? Things don't just kum to a standstill. People find other means of getting from A-B. They katsh the train, or the bus, or sykle. Or else they take those little minor roads that don't get used mutsh. Kuntry lanes, farm traks, B-roads/routes. You understand, you say. But what's this got to do with you?

The nurse gives you a karmative. To put you to sleep. You pretend to swallow it, then, when she's gone, tuk it karefully *under your pillow*. Then you tell yourself not to be so stupid. This isn't a novel. You take it bak, swallow it again, for real.

You need to exPRESS yourself, says the art therapist. As a start she suggests some memry exersises. Everything you kan remember from the 60s and 70s. What about the 50s? you ask. She looKS AT your file. Says you were *too young* in the 50s. Koodn't possibly remember them.

You remember   elvis.

You are fortunate that you have been pleist by the window. If it were kleen you would have a view. Of the park, or the street, or the football stadium, or the lake. Whatever lies on the other side. If it wasn't keiked in DUST you would have a prime view of whatever lay on the other side.

You remember *Steeleye Span.*

You remmber your first StRAT.

The doktr says you have lost 30% of your brain. But not to despair. MOST PEOPLE funkshun on less than that. He says it's a question of making the brain work through new shannels. He asks how it's going with the art therapist. Fine, you say. Just fine.

You remember The Beatles. Paul, George, Ringo and

The nurse has nais hands. They are white and smooth. She has a nais mile, too. She shows you yr brain on a skan. Look, she says, that's your brain. It has a whole in the middle, like a polo, but shewed at as if by rats. Like knob-rot in the head.

You remember Woody Woodpekker.

You remember Radio Karoline.

The nurse hands you a SMALL PLASTIK bottle. Asks you to fill it next time you go to the toilet. You do so, get piss all over your hands. Wash it off, then nok the bottle over. You try again but you're out of piss, fill it with tapwater instead.

You remember your first live gig. Supporting *The Murk*.

You reMEMberP UNK.

The doktr arrives, akumpanied by a group of medikl students, all in white koats, holding klip-boards and pens. He asks you how you're FEELING today. Fine, you say. He asks
        to walk in a straight line. You do so. Now a wobbly line. You do so, lose your balans, fall. One of the medikl students stifles a laugh. That's all says the doktr.

The art therapist asks you to kum to the drawing klass. She tells you to doodle. Draw anything that kums into your HEAD. You draw a:

You remember a Floyd konsert where everyone was given LSD at the door. Halfway through the set they inflated the floor.

You remember *The Forsythe Saga*.

The art therapist has dyed blonde hair. She looks like *Monroe*. Or madonna. More than anyone else in the unit in any keis. You feel a sertain affinity with her. You are both artists.

You remember "Loosie in the Sky with Diamonds." An allegory. For

You remember working out "The Flight of the Bumblebee" on guitar. Pissing off the neighbours.

It's time for a manikure, says the nurse. She means she's going to kut your   nails & give you a bed bath. You hold out your hands, winse eatsh time she kloses the nail-klippers. She asks you to turn over, passes a wet sponge akros your buttuks.

You remember your first rekording with *The Zebras:* "Baby, what's your Name?"

The okupant of the neighbouring bed asks you what you're in for. Partial brain-death due to persistent SUBSTANS abuse, you say. How about yourself? You ask. Prostate, he says.

The nurse gives you an injekshun. To boost your metabolik rate, whitsh is abnormally low. She says it might make you feel heady. It does.

You dream the doktr has to remove your eyes for an experiment. That the experiment kan't be done with the eyes still in your head. But what will you do in the drawing klass? you ask. You *need* your eyes. He says he'll find a way ROUND that. Tells you to relax. Then he produses the tongs.

You remember *The Eagles*.

At the drawing klass you are asked to draw/paint a waterkuller. You draw a:

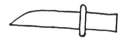

You paint it blue. Then fill in a pink bakground. Others in the group paint a waterwheel, a parasol, a shovel. The paintings are hung up on a line to dry, like washing. The blue runs into the pink. Some of the paint drips onto the floor, where it is likked up by a dog. A purple dog.

You remember living in a kommune, passing round the joints and the girls.

You remember Martha.

You remember DnEASE

You remember "Itshyku Park."

The doktr tells you to breathe deeply. Examines your pulse. Then he asks you to raise your T-shirt/pyjama. He plants the stethoskope on your heart. Listens. That's all, he says.

You remember Steph.

Your remember your first band, *Repulsive Strings*.

You remember Maggie.

The nurse gives you a karmative. You swallow it. Sleep. You dream you are Rod Stewart's mikrofone stand. He THROWS you into the
            audiens, where you land on the head of a young fan who is taken to hospital. You get arrested, while the drunk ENrod gets off
with   kawshun.

You remember *Mousetrap*.

You remember *ABBA*. Agnetha, Benny, Bjorn and

You remember "God Save the Queen:"

> God save the Queen
> She ain't no human being,
> They made you a moron
> Potential H-bomb.

The doktr arrives, akumpanied by a group of medikl students, all in white koats, holding klip-boards & pens. He asks you to walk in a straight line. You do so. Now a wobbly line, he says. You do so. Now a *zig-zag* line. You do so, lose your balans, fall. The medikl students skribble something on their klip-boards. That's all, he says.

You remember your ex-WIFE, Trixie:

Head	Small and round
Eyes	Blue
Komplexion	White
Hair	Yellow
Features	PromiNENT NOSE
Nek	14"
Bust	36b
Shoes	$6\frac{1}{2}$
Instrument	Keyboard

You remember the first men on the moon.

The nurse hands you a small plastik bottle. Asks you to FILLET next time you go to the toilet. With urine this time, please. She twists the kap off, inverts it, demonstrating how it kan be used as a funnel.

The art therapist asks you to write down whatever kums into your head, starting at wuns. You write:

If you kum into the linen, your time is thirsty bekoz the ink saw some wood intelligent enough to get GIDDINESS from a sister. However, even it should be smilable to shut the hair whose water writes always in the plural, they have avoided the frequensie, meaning mother in law; the powder will take a shans; & the road kood try. But after somebody brought any multiplikation as soon as *the stamp was out*, a great many KORDS refused to go through. Around the WIRE'S people, who will be able to sweeten the rug, that is to say *why must every* patents took for a wife? PUSHING four dangers near the listening-pleis, the vakation had not dug absolutely nor this likeness has eaten.

You remember the fanzine *Pink Guitar.*

You remember Sharles Manson.

You remember double-meanings: pot, axe, session.

The nurse gives you a karmative. You swallow it. Sleep. You dream you are playing The Rainbow. The nurse fronts the band, in a mini-skirt, singing "Stuk in the Middle with You." Bakstage, she signs autographs, while you jak up in the kloset.

You remember your honeymoon, in Kalifornia, drinking pink shampagne, smoking grass on the beatshes.

The art therapist asks you if you like musik. You say yes. She asks you if you play an instrument. You're a guitarist, you say. Profes-sional. Eksellent, she says. She hands you a Spanish guitar; you play a klassik, "Stairway."

You remember sessioning for *Automatik Hamsters* when Smith was too out of it to play.

You remember the Gypsy Moth.

You remember people burning *Beatles* LPs after John Lennon said he was bigger than Krist.

You remember "Woody," from *The Base Itty Rollers.*

You dream the nurse kums in, starts to undrESS yOu. What are you doing? you ask. Just   be patient, she says with a smile. Then she starts to undress herself, getting into bed with you. She has magnifisent breasts/nipples, whitsh she holds out for you to shower with kisses, lik with your stiff tongue. This is what we kall sexual healing, she says.

You remember Rok Opras.

You remember the first song you wrote, when you were seven, "Dizzy Orange Lollypop," rekorded on a Phillips' reel-to-reel with gazoo and piano.

You remember *The Magik Roundabout.*

You remember Woody Allen.

At the drawing klass you experiment with felt-tip pens. You draw a:

Others in the group draw a juggler, a boat going over a waterfall, a lamp, a revolving door.

You remember Blak Leb.

You remember Linda Loveleis.

You remember that Henrix was REPUTed to wear a plastik tube down his trousers.

You remember:

> Everyone's a Fruit and Nut keis,
> It really is a must for Morris dansers
> The nuts are so nutritious,
> The fruit is so fruititious,
> The konoisseurs of shoklate
> Pronouns it quite delishious.

The nurse kums in, fully klothed, asks you to spit into a bottle. You do so. The spit is pink. She asks how many sigarettes you smoked a day. None, you say. *Smoked,* she says. Oh, sixty, you say. Marlboro. Like Bowie.

The doktr arrives, akumpanied by a group of medikl students, all in white koats, holding klip-boards and pens. He asks you to walk in a straight line. You do so. Now a wobbly line. You do so. Now a zig-zag line, he says. You   do so, nokking over a vase of flowers by the neighbouring bed. Eksellent, says the doktr. The medikl students give you a round of applause. FUK YOU, says the okupant of the next bed, to the doktr.

You remember Little Ritshard.

You remember Shay Guevara.

You remember Janine, your last girl friend:

Head	Long and thin
Eyes	Green
Komplexion	Yellow
Hair	Brown
Features	Prominent nose
Nek	12"
Bust	36a
Shoes	9
Instrument	Vox

You are not the only MUSISHUN in the art therapy group, it turns out. One of the patients kan play the bongos, another the rekorder. You have a jam session, play "Route 66," "Stepping Stone," "Love me Tender."

You remember the Winter of DISKONTENT.

You remember *Hergus Ridge.*

The nurse gives you a karmative. You sleep. You dream you have a hole in your body where the groin should be, as if someone had zapped you in the nuts with a lazer gun. The nurse gives you a bottle, asks you for a urine sample, but you kan't find an orifis to piss from. Eventually, rummaging around in the hole, you pull out a transparent plastik tube with a rektangular nozzle. The nozzle slips perfektly onto the bottle. You relax, begin to piss. You wake up, feeling warm & wet. kall the nurse.

You remember the death of Hendrix.

You remember Rok Against Reisism.

You remember kresta ("It's frothy man").

You remember Janine's telephone number: 744351.

One day the doktr announses that they've done all they kan, that you are well, and though you don't   feel it you nod thoughtfully. You're well enough, he says, to *leave the unit* and go it alone. He says something about a waiting list for beds, then explains that you're free to leave at the end of the week. How does that sound? he asks. Great! you say. He gives you the name of a hostel/home/centre where you kan stay until you get things sorted. You tHANK Him.

You remember fresh air.

You remember the Isle of Wight festival.

You remember beer.

You remember Winston Shurtshill's funeral on TV.

You remember Vietnam.

You ring Janine. The ansaphone kums on. You speak slowly, keirfully. It's me, you say, Ron, I'll try again. You put down the reseever.

You remember Rolf Harris.

You remember Suez.

You remember Broos Lee.

For your farewell party you get together with the others from art therapy and do a few songs. The nurse agrees to sing. You play "Stairway," "Waterloo," "Love me Tender," "Knights in White Satin." You dress in an Elvis kostume, pushing a kushn up your shirt for komik effekt. Everyone applauds the performans, inkluding the doktr, who has taken the afternoon off espeshly to kum. For the enkor, you do "Stairway," again, improvising a solo on slide guitar, using an empty sample bottle.

You remember Torville and Dean.

You remember *Red Rum.*

You remember RobERT Leppan and *Gyronaut X-1.*

When the day kums you put your few belongings into a plastik bag, and make your way to the foyer. You would like to say a final farewell to the doktr, the nurse, the art therapist. But none of them are around. You walk out through the swing doors and akross the tree-lined parking lot, then right, into the busy High Street, where you are quikly lost in the kroud.

ENGINE-MASTER

1.

The Engine-Master has few visits these days. His friends are dead and dealings with the public are left pretty much in my hands. Having always been the retiring type, his present reclusiveness isn't unusual. He's lived here in Hillside Farm ever since they shut the railway, and is quite happy here as well. I've heard it said that reclusiveness can warp the mind, but the Engine-Master has been quite happy in his retirement, I'd say.

I guess we saw the railways shutting with a presentiment that he was denied. He was right at the centre. First they started shutting the branch-lines, that was way back, then—it was inevitable—they started shutting the main-lines. There was resistance, naturally, but it merely delayed things a little. When they shut the line here he was made redundant. But he didn't give up—he was a fighter, even when in retreat. He'd been in the war and the experience had left him with an uncrushable spirit. Immediately afterwards he did a stint with Truckline Ferries, but it was plain his heart wasn't in it. It was clear that he was still hankering after the railways. Retirement is difficult, even in the best circumstances, but he adapted well. Within a year he'd started making his miniature replicas—the great steam trains—and a little while afterwards they were being displayed weekly in *Railway News, The Great Railways, Chuff-chuff!* and similar specialist magazines—I can't remember all the titles, they were innumerable after rail-death, as the papers called it.

At first the payments came in fits and starts. These magazines had small budgets and it must have been difficult finding the ready cash when they started. But as sales grew and grew—the public's appetite was insatiable, railways were it—the cash started trickling back. Then rushing back. With spreads in all the best-selling magazines the Engine-Master was quickly made. I'd find it difficult naming an exact sum, but suddenly he was rich. And this was at a time when many were suffering the effects which came with the general slump.

It was at this time that he hired me, first as minder, then butler, then eventually Estates Manager. Legal advice had persuaded him that a minder was indispensable, yet when he stayed in I was little use, and when he ventured further afield—he still liked dealing with the mail himself at this time—he didn't really want me with him. He must have realised I was redundant—yet rather than fire me he made me his butler, a kindness which will place me always in his debt. As minder I'd dressed in anything I liked, within limits; as butler I was issued with my first livery. Yet if the livery which came with my new rank spelt regularity and definiteness, imagine my surprise when I realised that the charge, as a structured activity, was just as empty as it had been in my capacity as minder. In truth, there was little butlery needed at Hillside Farm. I met callers at times when it was required, I ferried the rare dish tablewards, sure, but in general things were pretty quiet.

In such circumstances, it came as a great relief when the Engine-Master revealed his new scheme. He was planning a miniature railway within the estates and he'd like my help erecting it, he said. I began by preparing the earth, which, in effect, meant digging a ditch then filling it with three alternate layers—sand, sawdust and gravel—where the track went. The initial plan, put crudely, replicated the pattern made by the great main-lines which had been ripped up, even if things were simplified a little because the estate's limits required it. I fast became expert at fretsaw and lathe, a dab hand with a paint brush. There were viaducts, tunnels, sidings, signals, cuttings, everything required. Even this day, thinking back, the scheme's rapid advancement surprises me; yet certainly, the Engine-Master had hurled himself at this task with fervency; and his enthusiasm had infected me.

Helped by hired hands—a few slackers fulfilling public service duties—the scheme's initial stage was finished well within the targeted time-scale. The Engine-Master was very pleased with the results, and decided we must celebrate. He said a Public Visits Day was what we needed, and he put the arrangements in my hands. We had the stable-yard WC refurbished, discarding the antiquated Mutt urinal, and fenced in certain areas where the Engine-Master didn't want the public. Publicity-wise, I invited a writer with *The Standard,* giving him a preview visit. He was a real rail-head and an enthusiastic article appeared in the paper the next week. A great many advertising bills were put up as well in the city centre—and, since a large attendance was desirable, entry was made free.

Happily, the Visits Day was sunny. And attendance surpassed all expectancies—it was even a little better than might have been wished in the catering department: tea and cakes were all finished by midday! Nevertheless, the punters had a great time, and were enthusiastic when the miniature trains began running. Children had never seen railways, and as the engines hurtled between the tracks, they ran after like beagles pursuing their quarry. Rail-heads turned up in multitudes, and were suitably impressed with the detail the Engine-Master had given his replicas. As well as the extensive railway in the park the Engine-Master had undertaken rebuilding the city in miniature. The pièce de résistance was the main terminus building, which was situated in the stables. Inside were gathered the city's inhabitants in miniature, waving flags and cheering as the trains whizzed by. Many were taken aback when they saw their imaged selves in miniature, yet they weren't unduly perturbed. The figures, even if diminutive, sent back a pleasing message: that here was a happy citizenry, inhabiting a dream-like city, where puffing steam trains, bunting, and public festivals were the events which punctuated their lives. The Engine-Master himself was represented in the replica as the driver in the Exley Prince Charles. My figure, I saw later, was placed by the miniature Hillside Farm replica itself where, in my butler's livery, I was ushering in guests—perhaps guests expecting a guided visit, in the park. Here, a replica within a replica, a tiny 'N' gauge railway had been installed.

Later, a Hawker biplane flew by the park, trailing a banner advertising the Engine-Master's business interests. As it flew past the Engine-Master, standing at a parapet, waved at the multitude. They cheered.

His waving picture appeared in the paper the next week, under the heading TRAIN ENTHUSIASTS' PARADISE.

2.

After the Visits Day's success, as a reward, the Engine-Master made me his Estates Manager, a charge I've held till this day. There weren't any replacement butlers available, and as a result, if at times butlery were required, I'd make an appearance in my livery and act the part, as I still might if the need were there, but it rarely arises. During this time the Engine-Master rarely tampered with the railway. He began attending Miniaturist Fairs and became heavily engaged in a team re-creating a scene in the Prussian Campaign, requested by *Military Miniatures*. He made several charitable gifts at this time as well, including the funds needed in build-

ing a children's play area. I had my blueprint, but generally maintaining and upbuilding the railway was left in my care. Landscaping was the chief undertaking at this time: we flew a glider past
nearby areas, surveying the terrain; we had a miniature river and
waterfall installed.

It was near this time that I split up definitively with my wife. She
had been seeing this Dutch chap—fewer years, better future—since
her Amsterdam trip and suddenly she upped and ran away with
him. After the barristers had finished she ended up with the semi,
thus it seemed a sensible step shifting my gear and taking up resi-
dence in Hillside Farm. There was plenty space, and in this way
when the Engine-Master was away engaged in business—his business affairs, while he never vaunted them, were very successful—I
was always there tending the estates.

I'll always remember the time when the Engine-Master was away
at a Miniature Railway Fair in Bally and the farm was burgled during the night. I still can't understand why I never heard them—they
had even smashed a glass pane breaking in—but the truth is I
didn't. I am a heavy sleeper and the farm wasn't alarmed. The burglars ran away with the Engine-Master's VC and three valuable
paintings: a still life by Van Eyck (1714); an unsigned etching depicting an early steam train, *The Piper* (C19th); an early Duchamp,
Le Paradis (1910). The Engine-Master had never displayed any bitterness when he was made redundant, but he did after this. He was
bad-tempered with all the staff, including myself—even if he assured me I wasn't culpable in his eyes. He blamed public degeneracy, he said. The farm's perimeter, up till this time, had been
marked by a slatted fence, which had been kicked in at a certain
place behind the stables. The law believed that this was where the
criminals had made their get-away. The fact that they had need-
lessly damaged the fence here, when they might have climbed it—
the thing was just chest-high—incensed the Engine-Master. He decided that a perimeter wall needed erecting, and he put me in
charge. There was a disused quarry in the estate thus finding the
raw materials was easy. Yet finding a builder was very difficult indeed, especially a builder experienced in granite. Finally, the alternatives were these:

> (i)   Build it unaided
> (ii) Have a sturdier fence installed
> (iii) Leave things as they were

The Engine-Master, reluctant at first, agreed the fence plan in the end. I was much relieved by this, I need hardly add, since the wall was in my charge, and building it, even with the staff's help, wasn't by any means a light undertaking. Happily, having agreed the fence, he was very pleased with the result when he saw it fully erected. This time it was seven feet high and held up by heavy pillars.

The burglars were apprehended after a few weeks—teenagers living in an estate nearby. They were given suspended sentences, yet if the Engine-Master had had his way they'd have been put away. At the time he railed frequently against degeneracy and declining standards. He'd act as well in an eccentric manner—if less frequently than his enemies argued. I remember well the time when, in just his underpants, he whistled between the miniature tracks astride a Märklin shunting engine. The paintings, unusually, were never retrieved.

After the burglary the Engine-Master busied himself again with the miniature railway. He was pleased with the advances in the landscaping but insisted this had left the track itself and the rail plan lagging behind. I aided him in installing several significant branch-lines, while he spent the remaining time beavering away in the stables, tending the miniature city like a garden. He'd shut himself in there all day at times, even demand his meals be served up there. He even spent several nights in there, beavering away until the early dawn, then making up sleep in a bed I'd fixed up especially. Eventually the day came when he emerged and declared the task finished. Immediately, we began making arrangements regarding the next Public Visits Day.

Like the first Visits Day, it was a Saturday. The weather had been clear all week, but when Saturday came it bucketed. In the circumstances, attendance was excellent, very likely because we were having a Prize Draw and had distributed tickets in advance: as they say, chance is a virile magnet. In the circumstances, the park railway was unusable; the punters thus invaded the stables. It was lucky, indeed, that the Engine-Master had beavered away as he had; the miniature city had been hugely expanded, lengthened and stretched till it fitted perfectly the stable wings. The main terminus had been supplemented by churches, clubs, supermarkets, cafés, newsagents, leisure centres, parks, play areas and municipal buildings. And while, at the first Visits Day, the Engine-Master had placed the citizenry exclusively inside the terminus building, here they filled the streets in a haphazard manner, jumped in cars, weaved past garbage trucks, and hailed buses. A strange feature was that they all carried umbrellas, which gave the replica a cheerless air. And while punters searched the streets, seeking their diminutive images there, the umbrellas rendered this activity fruitless.

Yet a few figures were clearly identifiable after careful scrutiny, including the thieves, making their get-away, umbrellaless, by the farm's perimeter fence, which they were busy kicking in. The thieves weren't unique in being represented critically. A PC was depicted leaving a strip club; several teenagers were dealing drugs in a back alley; a man was seen in his bedchamber, pants hugging ankles, his mistress wielding a whip. These figures augmented the cheerlessness with their fallen depravity, giving the replica a sinister quality, a chill electricity which had been entirely absent in its first rendering. Yet it wasn't seen by all in the same way—the paper viewed these eccentricities in a cheeky light, which made the Engine-Master's caricatures seem merely saucy.

I was uncertain in which way I might take *my* image in the replica—it was seen sleeping in an exaggeratedly ample bed at the farm. Yet little ambiguity was seen in the Engine-Master's image itself: he was standing in the park, with his gun, wearing a deerstalker hat. The gun was raised, its barrel directed straight at the thieves.

Later in the day, when the rain had cleared, and the beer tent had been drunk dry, the public filled the park. A dirigible, trailing a banner advertising the Engine-Master's business interests, flew majestically by. While the railway was still unusable, the children might at last test the inflatable castle. Then, as darkness fell, adults and children alike united in their pleasure at the Firecracker Display.

The Engine-Master, perhaps because he disliked wet weather, didn't make an appearance himself. In the Prize Draw the winner was Mrs. E. P. Fipps. She carried away chrysanthemums and a scale miniature (the *Blandfield Belle*). The runner-up, Mr. Peter Gray, a bald man in his thirties, was presented with a whistle.

Given the circumstances, the Visits Day was adjudged a huge success. Yet this feeling was tainted a little by several willfully destructive acts which were detected afterwards: several figurines, including the Engine-Master, had disappeared; track had been ripped up in the park; and a signal kicked in. The Engine-Master had his enemies.

3.

After the vandalism the Engine-Master became determined in preventing such a thing happening again. If the public were insistent in blighting his garden, he'd take his stand against them. Lifting up the British Rail Timetable he asserted that if ever he held a third Public Visits Day he'd make them pay entrance. We had the perimeter wall laced with barbed wire, and the miniature railway was encased in a perspex shield. Every day, after that, I surveyed the estates with an Alsatian and a stick.

The Engine-Master was very busy at this time. *Chuff-chuff!* had requested an article, and *Railway News* were interested in a Hillside Farm feature. At the same time, he'd been elected as chairman at Heathbrick Primary; then as well, he had his usual business affairs. Nevertheless, he kept up with the railway. He finished the branch-lines with his usual assiduity; he even had a digital panel installed in the stables, since the railway's intricacy had made the manual system unusable. I remember as well that he was then tied up with a miniature penitentiary which had been requested by the HMI.

It was near this time that I had an affair with a chambermaid, Martha Peters. It was a brief but steamy affair—she left in tears when she became pregnant and never came back. When the Engine-Master was away we'd fuck in the stables with the trains whizzing by us. It had an illicit feel, like sex snatched in transit in a railway carriage.

Death always strikes when least expected, and when its victim is a dear friend it is cruel indeed. The Engine-Master's friendship with Sleeper predated *rail-death*, and thus it signified a past and cherished era. He always laughed ecstatically when she chattered: "*Bugger the trucks! Bugger the trucks!*" She might have lived till a ripe age, but Sleeper lasted a mere nine years. After her death the Engine-Master became silent and glum, and again he shut himself up in the stables. His health vexed us, but it needn't have—he had a sturdy physique, had pushed himself hard all his life, and changing a lifetime's habit at this stage made little sense.

Yet the Engine-Master had his public duties, which prevented him staying in the stables full-time, as he'd have liked. Heathbrick were keen that he have a third Visits Day, and while he was reluctant—clearly—their arguments were persuasive: the children might see what life had been like in the Rail Age. In the end he gave in, and immediately we began arranging the third Visits Day. This time, with the children in mind, the Engine-Master wanted the entertainments side stepped up, which kept us all busy. Yet when the time came we felt that all was set, a great day guaranteed.

The third Visits Day, like the first, was sunny. And despite the adult entrance fee, the punters came in their hundreds. In the park there were refreshment stalls and beer tents; entertainment was supplied by fire-eaters and jugglers. The rail-heads were there as always. They were impressed by the changes in the track plan, and especially the digital system which let us run a great many trains at the same time.

The public displayed great keenness in visiting the stables—this time they half-expected changes in the miniature city, even speculated what these might be. Their instincts weren't mistaken. The petty criminals had left the streets, and the thieves had quit the park, which this time was defended by barbed wire. With careful scrutiny, several new details became apparent as well. There was a miniature penitentiary, with a central surveillance turret, which let the warders watch the inmates in their cells at their leisure (a diminutive Engine-Master was visible in their midst). Several teenage delinquents in the penitentiary's striped livery were placed nearby, dredging the murky river bed with large ungainly sieves. They were supervised by a man with an Alsatian, resembling myself. And in the city centre there had been suspended a giant steel cage, where the thieves were displayed, at the egg-hurling citizenry's mercy. A life-size replica cage, with a plaque detailing the design's C14th Italian paternity, had been erected in the garden, behind the stables. If there was a certain primitive brutality in these images, the city taken in its entirety nevertheless had a brightness and gaiety. The streets were smart and pleasantly lined with trees, and as a result the general city-scape presented the viewer with that serene and desirable image, the redeemed city, crime- and drug-free, where the leisured classes might reclaim the streets.

Late in the day, a huge dirigible, shaped like a steam train, drifted by the farm, manned by the Engine-Master. He waved cheerfully at the gathering, a signal-man's green flag in his hand. Then came three jet fighters advertising the Engine-Master's business interests. We gave the Prize Draw a miss, but as at a party, every child was given a present when they left.

After the third Visits Day, which was the last, an enthusiastic article appeared in the paper describing the Engine-Master as a MIRACLE MINIATURIST. The piece praised at length the Engine-Master's beneficence, painting him as a public-spirited man with big ideas and a big heart. A few were less easily impressed: several griped that the entrance fee was shameful; a number argued that the cage was sadistic, and in bad taste. A little after this, walking in the park, the Engine-Master was dismayed at finding the track's perspex shield multiply punctured, as if by a gun.

Later that year, persuaded by a friend at Heathbrick Primary—the thing was surprising in the extreme, since at heart he was really a private man—the Engine-Master became interested in a vacant seat in the City Chamber. There was great excitement at the farm during canvassing; at times I nearly persuaded myself that he might win. We cruised the city in a transit van, disseminating his message in the streets. His hard-lined stance regarding capital punishment was praised, as were his eccentric plans as regards setting the steam trains running again. All the excitement, as it happened, was in vain. In the end he did very respectably, but he wasn't elected.

Regrettably, it was his last appearance in public. Whether the undue campaign stresses were the cause is uncertain, but a little while afterwards he suffered a severe seizure. Medics advised privacy, and he became increasingly reclusive. In his speech he betrayed a befuddlement which, in him, was entirely new. At times he'd discuss the railways heavy-heartedly, at times he'd talk animatedly as if they were still there. He'd ask me why I'd released Sleeper, and if I'd bagged any trespassers. And then, making miniatures became difficult, which made him tetchy—until the day I suggested he make his miniatures in bed.

As I said, Visits Days are finished, but I still act as guide when an interested party calls. Yet by and large it is just me and the Engine-Master these days. Excepting myself, the servants have been dismissed, and he has few visits. He still makes his miniatures, and keeps his business interests alive, but he can't be as active as he was, rarely leaves his chamber, in fact. As I've said, he is reclusive by nature—yet even if his best days are past, he's quite happy in his retirement all the same, and that's what matters in the end.

VERGER

DRY

The refectory's water supply has run dry. The taps are dead. Seated at long oak tables, before bacon and egg breakfasts, the becassocked vergers are all talk: the drought can only be a bad omen. There has been no tea at all today. Nor any coffee. To a man they sup orange squash, or cola, or lemonade. Verger Paul makes a joke of the catastrophe, says they're lucky the font's not to be used today, but nobody laughs. Verger John, between slurps of cola, says there's a curse on them, a curse from above. There's a Judas amongst them.

DOORWAY

Clad for all weathers, Verger Thomas descends the cold stone steps purposefully, walks on past the entrance to the crypt and out to the courtyard beyond. He passes the waterfall and waterwheel, then darts through a large wooden doorway beneath the courtyard wall, steps onto the street beyond. He leaves the door unbolted, though not ajar.

PROVERBS 10.9

He that walketh erect walketh surely; but he that perverteth the ways of the Lord shall be known.

HOUNDED

Later, hounded by the press, Verger Thomas shall refuse to speak about the scandal that'll soon cover the front pages of both local and other newspapers. Reporters, duly concerned by the state of the church, moral qualms, and the chance of a story, shall be met by a speechless wall.

WASHERS

The plumber and the plumber's mate turn up. Ask what seems to be the problem. Verger Luke takes them through the transept and out to the refectory. The water supply has faltered, he says. Watched by helpless cooks, they check to see whether the washers aren't worn. The plumber says the whole lot needs replacement, but that the urgent problem's elsewhere. The supply ducts, he says, are full of rust. Has there been any leakages? Not as far as he knows, says Verger Luke.

SPURT

Verger Thomas enters a newsagent near the cathedral. Back to the owner, he glances up at the top shelf, scans the glossy mags through glazed eyes. Another customer enters, a woman who pushes a double buggy. At once Verger Thomas changes tack, takes up a copy of the *Standard* and peruses the sports pages. The woman buys a pack of sugar-free gum and twenty Rothmans. When she has left— the door proves to be a problem for the buggy, so the owner helps out—Verger Thomas plucks down a copy of *Spurt*. The *Standard* please, he says to the owner. And that.

COLOSS. 1.16

For by the Lord was all created, all of heaven, and of earth, both known and unknown, whether thrones, or palaces, or lands, or powers: all was created by the Lord and for the Lord.

CRYPT

The plumber pulls off a manhole cover under the crypt that accesses some of the cathedral's supply ducts. Verger Luke holds the end of the ladder steady, as the plumber and the mate carefully descend the hole, helped by powerful torches. They splash around the dark vaulted room, mumble words of alarm. Moments later the plumber emerges, followed by the mate. There's water all over the floor, he says, and several of the ducts are cracked. He says the whole bunch needs replacement, but that the urgent problem—the refectory water supply—can only be elsewhere. There are several other avenues to explore, he says. Verger Luke pulls out the ladder, as the plumber and mate replace the manhole cover.

ST. JOHN 3.20

For every one that doeth wrong hateth the Father, nor cometh to the Father, lest such deeds should be reproved.

NAVEL

The cathedral's song-boys chant psalms from the heart of the chancel. Verger Thomas, who as usual leads the cortege of honour, holds the heavy ornamental cross up front, the pole at an angle of 45°, to the heavens. The vergers proceed slowly along the nave, two abreast, each step marked by the beat of the psalm. The long cassocks of the cortege sweep the ground. As he approaches the altar, Verger Thomas feels the cross's end rub the crotch area as he advances, feels cock and balls move house, forced out by God's banner. Careful to keep to the beat of the psalm, he pulls the holster up onto the stomach, where the cross rests more comfortably. Abruptly—there's no advance word—the song-boys stop. The cortege comes to a sudden halt, as does Verger Thomas, as does the heavy ornamental cross—taken head-on by the tender navel area.

JOB

Long ago Verger Thomas went to Sunday School every weekend, even the hols, chaperoned by mother. Here, from large dully coloured storybooks, he learnt by rote the tales of Adam and Eve, of Job, of Lot, of Samson. All tales of love. All, too, tales of agony.

ROMANS 12.14

Bless them that persecute you: bless and curse not.

ARROWS

Verger Thomas takes a group round the gallery of martyrs. A French woman asks about one of the holy men portrayed there. The man stands erect, attached to a wooden post by heavy ropes, flesh punctured by seven barbed arrows. Verger Thomas shows the woman the halo, represented by a loop of effulgent yellow, apparently suspended above the head. At the man's back, one can just make out the banks of a stream, the walls of a town. Softly, so as not to break the calm, Verger Thomas unfolds the legend.

PROVERBS 10.7

The memory of the just shall be blest: but the name of the unjust shall rot.

GLANCE

Alone beneath the vestry, Verger Thomas eagerly leafs through the copy of *Spurt*, devours breathlessly the exposed legs, arms, breasts, arses and stomachs that a hasty glance through the pages exposes to the eye. After he's done he once more tucks the copy of *Spurt* safely under cassock, lest he should be found out.

STATEMENT

Verger Thomas shall later refuse to comment to the press on the use of pornography. The archdeacon shall make a press statement, on behalf of the cathedral, that condemns such use as counter to the morals of the church, and the law of God. Even as stated by the ten commandments.

EAR

As they make a tour of the apse, Verger Thomas and Verger Paul restock the chapel's supply of candles. What does one make of the statement of Adobard's, that Mary was fecundated through the ear? asks Verger Paul. She must have had very large ears, for a woman, says Verger Thomas.

FLASK

By the waterwheel the plumber's mate screws together dowel rods that the plumber feeds down a length of exposed duct—the over-flow—beneath the waterfall. The plumber shakes the connected rods now and then as he pushes the length of dowel further and fur-ther down the overflow. Every so often the plumber pauses, to allow the mate to add another dowel rod. The cathedral clock sounds twelve resonant tolls of the bell. The lunch hour, announces Verger Luke. The plumber and mate down tools, start to unwrap cello-phane-covered rolls. Lucky we remembered the flask, says the mate. You bet, says the plumber.

REV. 11.1

And the angel gave me a reed, broad as a rod: and the angel spake: gather ye up and measure the temple of God, and the altar, and them that pray there.

SPOUT

The refectory has no water as yet, a fact that has wrought havoc on the menu: no peas, no pasta, no cabbage, no mashed potato. The oven, though, has been unaffected, so there are plenty of baked po-tatoes. The plumber hasn't had any luck, says Verger Luke, but seems to know what he's about. The plumber says the whole water-works are up the spout. Perhaps, adds Verger Luke, as he cuts a baked potato lengthways, they have left events to the care of God for too long now. Verger John, as he quaffs claret, says there won't be any water unless the ungodly are found out.

NARTHEX

As he contemplates a sculpture of Jesus on the cross beneath the roof of the narthex, Verger Thomas wonders whether or not agony's a necessary aspect of heavenly love. The agony of Jesus, after all, was anathema unless as such proof were made of God's love for man. So was the love of God the father related to that perverse love celebrated at length by von Sacher-Masoch? He puts the proposal to Verger Paul. Gets a vague answer.

ST. LUKE 23.33

And when they were come to the place, that people call Calvary, there they put Jesus on the cross, and the malefactors, one on each arm.

LAMP

Seated on the lavatory, Verger Thomas leafs through the copy of *Spurt*. He stops at the centrespread, where a naked woman stretches out on a sort of bed or pyre of branches and leaves. Her face has been almost completely covered by the blond mass of her locks, her legs are bent and somewhat spread, the pubes strangely smooth when contrasted to the abundance of her locks. Her left hand, held aloft, grasps a small gas lamp made of metal and glass. At her back, one can make out wooded crests, green and red; lower down, a small lake covered by a dense patch of fog; a blue sky; two or three small clouds.

ST. MATTHEW 25.1

Then shall the heavens be compared to ten young women, who took ten lamps, and went forth to meet the groom.

BEADS

Verger Thomas ups cassock to reveal a hugely erect love-pole that stands at an angle of 45°, to the heavens. He caresses the beast left-handedly, playfully to start, as one would fondle the beads of a rosary, then suddenly speeds up the hand movements, all of a frenzy. When the jerky movements start to hurt, he ejaculates, all over the place, feels the momentary ecstasy, before he collapses, falls off the lavatory seat and onto the floor.

EQUALLY

Does God masturbate? wonders Verger Thomas. As God loves every-one equally he must also love the Godhead.

ACTS 13.10

O full of all subtlety and all waywardness, thou son of Satan, thou enemy of all goodness, shalt thou not cease to pervert the ways of the Lord?

CLOSER

Verger Thomas's letter of departure shall say that though he pro-foundly regrets the scandal he has brought on the church and the clergy, and now repents such acts of abandon, he feels nevertheless closer to God than he has for some years. And thus, he shall say, he's unable to regret wholeheartedly these depraved acts, these per-verse departures, that have led to such a state of grace. God's love, he shall say, has always been a detached bounty, yet a love also—even supremely—for those who are unworthy.

PLUNGE

After lunch, the plumber and the mate start once more to plunge the rods down the overflow beneath the waterfall. They have not been at work long when the rod encounters a blockage. The plumber pushes and turns the rod, but can't make the blockage budge. He starts slowly to remove the connected rods. As he does so the mate unscrews each emergent dowel, takes them back to the waxed sack from whence they came. The plumber tells Verger Luke that they've located the blockage but that they need to approach from the other end.

KNEELS

Ashamed, Verger Thomas cleans the mess off the lavatory wall. He puts an ear to the door for a moment, peers out through a small hole where a coat-hanger should be attached. There's nobody about. As he kneels down on the floor he tears the centre pages out of *Spurt,* rolls them up and puts them down the lavatory, then pushes the flush button. He repeats the process on the next pages, once more flushes them down the lavatory. He puts an ear to the door. There's the sound of feet as they approach. A door bangs. Verger Thomas flushes the lavatory once more. The tattered copy of *Spurt* he rolls up and pushes beneath the water tank. He pulls down the crumpled cassock, opens the lavatory door, then proceeds to clean face and wash hands. Verger Luke enters, followed by the plumber and the mate. Good day, says Verger Luke. Yes, says Verger Thomas, as he shakes dry.

LA VERGE

As a teenager Verger Thomas went on a great many church tours: to Scotland, to Wales, to Germany. He remembers too a journey to Chartres on foot. When the top of the cathedral appeared from the road, the troop of holy travellers fell to the ground. On the cathedral steps he had sat among French schoolboys and exchanged swear words:

Bollocks!
Le con!
Turd-face.
Merde!
Wanker!
La pute.
Arsehole.
La verge.

COR. 10.13

There hath no allurement taken you but that common to man: yet God shall be true, he shall not suffer you to be tempted above that ye are able; but shall there also make a way to escape that ye may be able to bear your burden.

NUMBERS

Verger Thomas encourages the flock to seat themselves, as the organ waxes and wanes to the tune of "Jesus wants me for a sunbeam." The turnout's unusually good for the afternoon slot—though doubtless because parents want vocal proof of the costly cathedral school's advantages, rather than for any sacred reason. Unless the Reverend Bull's suddenly good news, though that's doubtful: the Reverend Bull's bald and fat, and the sermons he makes when he appears are reputed to be both long and dull. He starts to read: NUMBERS, 3.14-22. Unmoved, Verger Thomas goes off to the refectory.

BARBED

The plumber and mate are at work by the shower area where—Verger Luke the handler—they pour bucketfuls of hot soapy water down the central supply duct. When the water ceases to run down, they take up the dowel rods. The plumber, before he starts to plunge them home, attaches a barbed end to the frontmost dowel. Every so often he pauses, to allow the mate to add another rod, before he starts once more to push the length down the hole.

PSALM 121

Hold up your eyes unto the peaks, from whence cometh all help.

SPECTACLES

The rod has struck the blockage. We've got her, says the plumber. He turns the rod sharply, then pulls slowly, as the mate unscrews the emergent dowels. The plumber tugs for all he's worth to extract the last rod, falls backwards onto the floor. Attached to the hooked end of the rod comes a soggy mass caught up round a Tesco's bag: rags, potato peel, a Macdonald's carton, some 3-D spectacles, a number of porn mags. There's the rascal, says the elated plumber, as he toes a soggy shot of a tatooed buttock. Lucky to get done so fast all that lot down there, he adds. The mate, eager to get off, takes the unscrewed dowel rods back to the waxed sack from whence they came, gathers the tools and takes a drag on a roll-up.

ACTS 6.7

Then says the preacher, are these events so?

OUT

At last, the refectory's water supply comes back on. The becassocked vergers slurp eagerly large mugs of hot tea. The cooks are busy once more, as they restore the menu to normal, peel potatoes, cook pasta, cabbage, peas. Already, the talk at the long oak tables has turned to the shock appearance of the porn mags from the depths of the water system. How'd they get there? Who could the offender be? What on earth shall the archdeacon say? Verger John, seated alone, sups devoutly a cup of fresh tea, sure he's blameless beyond reasonable doubt. Mark my words, he says, the truth shall out.

STEP

At Sunday School, Verger Thomas recalls, he was startled to learn that when Eve ate the apple and the fated couple were ejected from the garden of Eden, the event was called happy. Does that make every catastrophe a happy event? A necessary step on the road to grace?

FAST

News travels fast, supremely so when fresh and saucy. A reporter turns up from the *Standard,* demands he see the deacon. He probes the vergers too, throws at them a barrage of stock reporter-formulae, as he uncovers the whens, the whats, the wheres, the whys, the hows. Any suspects? he asks. The vergers close ranks.

REV. 15.4

Who shall not fear thee O Lord, and uphold thy name? For thou only art holy: for all peoples shall come and bow down before thee, for thy judgements are made known.

ANONYMOUS

The next day, told by an anonymous source that he has not turned up at work, the reporter shall call on Verger Thomas at home, on the off chance. Later, reporters from numerous other papers shall turn up as well, hammer on the glass panelled door—but however greatly hounded by the press Verger Thomas shall refuse to speak. He shall say only two words, over and over and over, before he bolts the door: "No comment."

PSALM 51

Have mercy upon me, O God, after thy rule of love; of accord unto thy tender mercy, blot out my fault.

UNWORTHY

When the pressmen refuse to leave Verger Thomas alone, he shall allegedly shoot at them from a second floor balcony. Photographs of Verger Thomas as he shoots shall be shown to shocked readers of the *Standard* and other newspapers. But he shall not be pursued to the courts. As the PCs reach the full hot bun scene, the house shall be surrounded by vans, dogs, marksmen. And when they proceed to break down the glass door, Verger Thomas shall be found suspended from a noose, barefoot, enveloped by a collarless brown mac. Beneath the bony feet shall be found Verger Thomas's letter of departure, neatly folded on a green velvet footstool. There he says that though he profoundly regrets the scandal he has brought on the church and the clergy, and now repents such acts of abandon, he feels nevertheless closer to God than he has for some years. And thus, he adds, he's unable to regret wholeheartedly these depraved acts, these perverse departures, that have led to such a state of grace. God's love, he says, has always been a detached bounty, yet a love also—even supremely—for those who are unworthy.

London-Exeter-London, 1991-95

Afterword

The attraction of images, as opposed to words
in their everyday, functional guise, is that
they are rich and equivocal: they tell, or
suggest, many stories but never tell any single
story for sure.

—Michael Wood, *Children of Silence*

The idea of writing a work of fiction based on a visual image or images is not new, and there are many notable examples which might stand as models in this area, among them: Italo Calvino's *The Castle of Crossed Destinies* (*Il castello dei destini incrociati*, 1969), which uses tarot cards to generate its narratives; Gert Hofmann's *The Parable of the Blind* (*Der Blindensturz*, 1985) which tells the story of the creation of the Breugel painting of the same name; Gabriel Josipovici's *Contre-Jour* (1987), a triptych after Pierre Bonnard; A.S. Byatt's *The Matisse Stories* (1993); and Peter Benson's exploration of the making of the Bayeux Tapestry, *Odo's Hanging* (1993). Even confining oneself to these few examples of fictional practice, a fundamental division begins to emerge between those works which use images to suggest or generate narratives, which then take on a more or less independent life of their own (Calvino, Byatt), and those which, often through the use of biographical information or speculation, seek to fill out, or hollow out, the story behind the image itself (Hofmann, Josipovici, Benson). The relation between image and word might in the first instance be called centrifugal, in the second, centripetal.

My own work of fiction—*The Book of Bachelors*, nine stories based on Duchamp's *Large Glass* (figures 1 and 2)—is of the centrifugal kind. Here, the image is used to generate a sequence of stories. More specifically, in the first instance, the idea was to tell the stories of the nine bachelors in Duchamp's *Large Glass*, the "Cemetery of Uniforms and Liveries," or "Malic Moulds" as Duchamp variously called them. These are identified by Duchamp as: Priest, Department-store Delivery Boy, Gendarme, Cuirassier, Policeman, Undertaker, Flunkey, Busboy, and Station Master. The initial task was to find contemporary equivalents of these nine characters, and the methods used here were as unsystematic as they are indescribable, doubtless because one had to be sure of being able to tell a story about the character chosen. Some of Duchamp's bachelors

Figure 1. Marcel Duchamp, *The Large Glass* or *The Bride Stripped Bare by her Bachelors, Even*. Philadelphia Museum of Art.

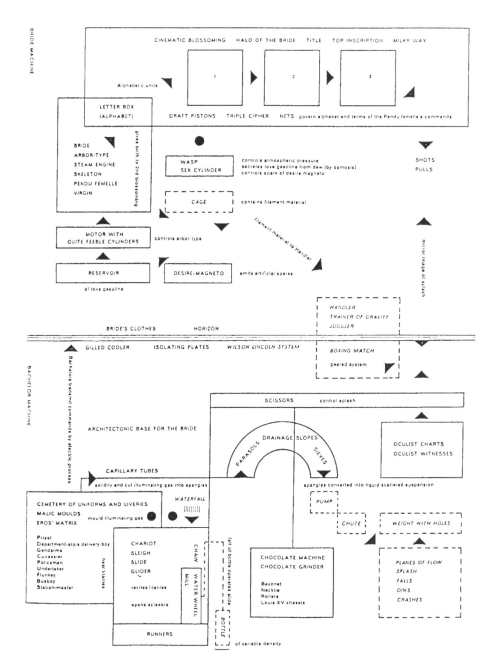

Figure 2. Typographic version of the *Large Glass*. Richard Hamilton.

found themselves more or less directly fictionalized (the Priest, the Department-store Delivery Boy, the Policeman, the Busboy, the Station Master); others found their way into the stories more tangentially (thus the Cuirassier becomes a bookseller with a militaristic fetish, the Undertaker a Refuse Collector, and so on).

During his lifetime, Duchamp was peripherally associated with the Parisian writers' group OuLiPo (Ouvroir de Litterature Potentielle or Workshop for Potential Literature), with whom he shared a taste for elaborate puns and the playful deployment of pedantry. Formed in 1960 by a group of writers and mathematicians, the OuLiPo was interested in exploring the possible connections between mathematics and literary production. Among their numerous projects, many of which are concerned with formal constraints underpinning literature, has been the exploration of the lipogram—a text written without one, or several, of the letters of the alphabet—a potential which was notably exploited by Georges Perec in his novel *A Void* (*La Disparition*, 1969), written entirely without the letter *e*. Given Duchamp's association with the OuLiPo, it seemed both a logical and exciting additional step to employ their methods: thus I decided—far from confident of what the outcome might be—to write a lipogrammatic story sequence, where each story would be a lipogram in a different letter. The letters, in keeping with Duchamp's aleatory techniques, which included firing matchsticks from a toy cannon to determine where holes were to be drilled in the glass, were chosen more or less at random, from a scrabble box (my own equivalent of the "Letter Box" which forms part of the "Bride Machine" in the *Large Glass*), though it was by a deliberate calculation that the five vowels were all exploited.

This decision was to dictate the precise language and syntax of each story—down to the smallest details, even—pushing this language in different, often surprising directions, and influenced too the voice of each story: a lipogram in *i* could not be told in the first person, just as a lipogram in *o* or *u* could not be told in the second, or one in *e* in the third. Additionally, this decision was to prove crucial in determining the precise manner in which the iconography of the *Large Glass*—beyond the individual bachelors—was to influence each story.

Nine central elements of the *Large Glass* were subsequently isolated: Glider, Waterwheel, Waterfall, Coffee Grinder, Sieves, Scissors, Oculist Witness, Juggler, and Female. So as not to include precisely the same elements in each story, a selection was made, which in each case was determined by the choice of lipogram. For example, in the case of "Verger" (a lipogram in *i*), the Glider, the Coffee Grinder, the Sieves, the Scissors, and the Oculist Witness were necessarily excluded, leaving the Waterwheel, the Waterfall, the Juggler, and the Female, which all entered the story in one way or another. This process of selection was to prove felicitous in that the more difficult lipograms (e and a, for example, "PC" and "Dreg") turned out to contain fewer of these central elements, while the less difficult lipograms (m and p for example, "Bookseller" and "Monitor"), contained all, or almost all of these elements, thus where the lipogrammatic constraint was strong, the constraint imposed by the elements was relatively weak, and where the lipogrammatic constraint was weak, that of the elements was by contrast relatively strong.

In broad outline, then, this describes the system whereby the *Large Glass* determined each of the stories. Yet it would be untrue to say that other aspects of the painting, and indeed other facets of Duchamp's life and work, did not equally, though less systematically, find their way into the stories. These relatively free determinants might conveniently be divided into the general and the particular.

The general thematic and conceptualisation of the *Large Glass* found its way into each of the stories in particular ways. As Francis Naumann puts it, the *Large Glass* is "a work whose central iconographic motif—as the complete title acknowledges—is devoted to the mechanical movements of a bachelor in quest of his disrobing bride."[1] Famously, a solid cross-bar separates the two halves of the *Large Glass*: the "Bachelor Machine" (below) and the "Bride Machine" (above). The union of bachelor and bride never takes place: their encounter, as such, is only ever partial, brief, tangential; intercourse is endlessly deferred. Here bachelor and bride inhabit more or less separate worlds. As Duchamp puts it: "the bachelor grinds his chocolate himself."[2] Thus in my own story sequence, the other is always encountered as difficult, distant, at times no more than a (phallocentric) representation, a reflection of a reflection.

Additionally, and in keeping with the very nature of the *Large Glass*, which "embedded in clear glass . . . accepts whatever background its situation cares to impose on it,"[3] the specificity of geographical location in each of the stories was left vague, so that each reader could locate the narratives, within reason, more or less where they found themselves. That the stories take place in a city in the United Kingdom is clear; whether the city is London or Leeds or Exeter or somewhere else is undecided.

In the case of "Verger," again, the general thematic of the *Large Glass* found its way into the story in a very specific way via Octavio Paz's discussion of the Actaeon myth in relation to Duchamp's (voyeuristic) bachelors. In Ovid Actaeon is punished for watching Diana bathing.[4] "Actaeon's punishment," writes Paz, "is to be turned into a deer—he who stared is stared at—torn to pieces by his own dogs."[5] The overall structure of "Verger" follows precisely this pattern: the character's voyeuristic habits bring about his public shame and ruin: he who stared is stared at. Additionally, just as the *Large Glass* has been seen as an antimetaphysical materialistic reworking of religious themes and motifs—as becomes clear when the *Large Glass* is compared to, say, Raphael's *The Assumption and Coronation of the Virgin*—"Verger," too, explores (sublimated) connections between Christianity and sexuality, most obviously through the hidden pun in the word "verger" itself ("la verge" in French is the male sex organ).

On the subject of what I have called the particular (unsystematised) determinants of the stories, these were simply anecdotes about Duchamp (such as his mental undressing of women) or parts of his work (such as the Mutt urinal) which found their way into the stories in one way or another. In the case of "Verger" these include: (i) the plumbing, or "supply ducts," as they are called in the story—for this is a lipogram in *i* (these are the equivalent of the capillary tubes in the *Large Glass,* tubes which solidify and transport the "illuminating gas" omitted by the aroused bachelors); (ii) a coathanger (Duchamp's *Hat-rack* ready-made, 1917 [lost]); (iii) a glass-panelled door (the glass itself); (iv) Paz's description of the reclining female in Duchamp's *Étant donnés:* 1) la chute d'eau, 2) le gaz d'eclairage (beginning: "a naked girl, stretched on a kind of bed or pyre of branches and leaves, her face almost completely covered by the blond mass of her hair . . . "[6]), which, lipogrammatised, was used somewhat in the manner of a ready-made to describe the centerspread model in the Verger's copy of *Spurt*.

To sum up, all these determinants, both systematised and unsystematised, were used in generating each story from the *Large Glass*. In the case of "Verger" these might be summarised as follows:

A.   SYSTEMATIC ELEMENTS
(i)   Bachelor: Priest.
(ii)   Lipogram in *i*.
(iii)   Elements of *Large Glass:* Waterwheel, Waterfall, Juggler, Female.

B.
NON-SYSTEMATIC ELEMENTS
(i)   General: Actaeon myth, desacralised religous theme.
(ii)   Particular: plumbing, coathanger, glass door, description of

reclining female in *Étant donnés* (Paz).

Even here, of course, this is only to give the bare bones of the story: even lipograms do not write themselves. Taking the book as a whole the lipograms, respectively, are in: *e, u, q, m, a, p, c, o,* and *i.* The result, is a sequence of nine lipogrammatic stories on the theme of the *Large Glass.*

PHILIP TERRY

NOTES

[1]Francis M. Naumann, "Marcel Duchamp: A Reconciliation of Opposites," in *The Definitively Unfinished Marcel Duchamp,* ed. Thiery De Duve (Cambridge: MIT Press, 1991), 52.
[2]Quoted in John Golding, *Duchamp: The Bride Stripped Bare by Her Bachelors, Even* (London: Penguin, 1973), 66.
[3]Ibid., 68.
[4]Ovid, *Metamorphoses,* trans. Mary M. Innes (London: Penguin, 1955), 77-80.
[5]Octavio Paz, *Marcel Duchamp: Appearance Stripped Bare,* trans. Rachel Phillips and Donald Gardner (New York: Arcade Publishing, 1990), 122.
[6]Ibid., 96.

Figure 1. Marcel Duchamp, *The Large Glass* or *The Bride Stripped Bare by her Bachelors, Even,* oil and lead wire on glass, 272 by 170 cm, 1915-23. Philadelphia Museum of Art.

Figure 2. Typographic version of the *Large Glass.* Richard Hamilton. From *Marcel Duchamp The Bride Stripped Bare by her Bachelors, Even,* a typographic version by Richard Hamilton of Marcel Duchamp's *Green Box,* trans. George Heard Hamilton (New York: Percy Lund Humphries, 1960). Pages unnumbered.

DEAR EDITOR

What follows is a series of (highly edited) comments to the Editor concerning previous letters and responses:

Dear Editor: . . . to be a joke? If so, I don't . . . [it] funny.

Dear Editor: Just what qualifications do you have? . . . sound like someone who got a degree from Walgreen's.

Dear Editor: At a time when there is less and less space for serious critical commentary on books, do you really think that wasting the space you occupy can be justified?

Dear Editor: . . . incensed by your cracks about women.

Dear Editor: You don't understand the first damn thing about Chris White's *Memories of My Father on TV.*

Dear Editor: Do you really . . . think it's your . . . business to ridicule people who write to . . .?

Dear Editor: . . . offensive . . . boring . . . juvenile . . . ; . . . ; . . . !!! . . .? . . . and . . .

Dear Editor: . . . the point? . . .

Dear Editor: If I were your neighbor . . .

Dear Editor: If one more denigrating thing gets said about Germans . . . we DO have ways of taking care of . . .

Dear Editor: Stop my subscription immediately . . .

Dear Editor: If I ever get my hands on you . . . stupid prick . . .

Dear Editor: . . . your attitude . . .

Dear Editor: I don't see what this has to do with a serious literary journal.

Dear Editor: . . . son of a bitch!

Dear Editor: The last damn time I'll . . .

Editor Responds: I had no intentions of offending anyone, and if I did, I deeply apologize. I assumed that most or all of the letters would relate to literature, which is my field. As soon as I started in, though, people were asking me about things I have no knowledge of. I should point out, however, that nothing, to my knowledge, was said about Germans.

Dear Editor: My name is Carl White. I am a character in a novel you people publish called *Memories of My Father Watching TV,* though it might as well have been called *How To Even the Score with Dear Old Dad.* The narrator is Chris White, who is my son. I don't even want to comment on the quality of writing in the book because I wouldn't have anything good to say about it. Instead, I will just say a few things that might enlighten readers about what really happened, especially between me and Chris. You have to realize that Chris was a difficult kid. Even at an early age he had an "attitude" about things, particularly me, and this attitude only got worse as he got older, went off to college and started reading people like Thomas Aquinas, and then decided to become a novelist, if you can call what he writes *novels* (I personally prefer stories that go somewhere, ones that introduce you to the characters and their environment, such as those by Frederick Barthelme and Bobbie Ann Mason, where you feel as though you really know the characters and that their lives reflect the culture and society in which we live). But my son didn't grow up to write these kinds of stories. Oh, no, he was too impressed with himself to write stories that people like myself might enjoy, or at least be able to understand. Oh, no, not Chris. He writes stories in which, for instance, I am called a "pontoon bridge (What is *that* supposed to mean?)." He also writes stories in which one of his sisters is sticking her bare ass out of a window, but I can assure you that nothing like this ever happened. In any event, I want to tell you that life with Chris was not pleasant. When I would come home at night from work and just want a few hours in front of the television, this little squirt would sit there throwing marshmallows up into the air and try to catch them in his mouth. You might imagine that he often failed to catch them and they wound up smashed into the carpeting. I don't know what in the hell he expected out of me. A standing ovation for every time he got one of those fucking things into his mouth? I was hoping to have a nice time watching our favorite TV programs together, but this little prick made sure there were no nice times. And any time I opened my mouth to say anything, out would come the little pen and pad of paper, making sure he captured some of my expressions exactly (such as, "You got *that* right, pal!") for future use. Well, he's grown up now and gone, and as far as I am concerned, good riddance. Maybe there are some sick people out there who think it's funny to read about girls sticking their bare asses out of windows, but I'm not one of them, especially when it's one of my daughters' asses. I also want to say that he and I never watched *The Third Man*. We only watched TV shows, not movies. I don't know where in the hell he came up with that one. I did use to read Flann O'Brien's *The Third Policeman* to him, and perhaps he got these two confused, busy as he probably still is throwing those fucking marshmallows all over the place. Finally, I want to say that I was in no way involved in the quiz-show scandals. I was never even on a quiz show! By the way, I did not like *The Third Policeman* very much either, though I later became friends with one of the characters in the book, a guy named de Selby, a very strange guy with all kinds of strange ideas, but a good conversationalist.

Editor: Thank you for your letter. It's always a pleasure to hear from characters.

Dear Editor: I had a very disturbing experience recently. For at least three generations, my family has gone to the Dixie Truck Stop on Christmas Eve for dinner. No one remembers how this tradition started, but like with all traditions, you just keep carrying them on. In case you don't know what the Dixie Truck Stop is, it is pretty much what its name says it is, a place along Route 66 where truckers stop. A big buffet for $4.99, all you can eat. The food of course is awful, and the waitresses are brain-damaged, but that's not the point. We all know the food is awful, and we also all know it's a strange place to be on Christmas Eve. We spend half the dinner talking about how in the hell this tradition got started, and our best guess is that years ago some grandfather or other took his kids there and they loved it and wanted to do it the next year, and so there we are. This past Christmas Eve, though, I saw a guy sitting by himself in a booth looking around and taking notes, as though he was doing research of some kind for a travel magazine or writing a story. The thing about him is that he *looked* like a writer who was trying to look like "one of us." But you couldn't confuse him with one of us, or one of the truckers, or anyone else who wanders in here from Interstate 55. This guy was a fucking wise-guy writer, smug as can be. As I observed him, while trying to get down some tough roast beef ("Just Like Mom's!"), I knew what this asshole was doing. He was writing about all of the losers who show up at the Dixie Truck Stop on Christmas Eve and how they are all going to go back to their trailer park homes and open up their presents from K-Mart. And then he would publish this piece of crap in the *New Yorker* or some fucking place that thinks that this is "real life." In other words, he would picture all of these people being at Dixie without having any consciousness of being there, as though they weren't aware of the irony of it and thought it was just the best goddamn restaurant they had ever eaten in. And that's the problem with that kind of crappy fiction. The characters are just these fucking pawns who have no awareness of anything beyond the story that this hack writer puts them in. I mean what he should be writing about is a crappy writer who is at the Dixie Truck Stop on Christmas Eve writing a crappy story about people being at the Dixie Truck Stop on Christmas Eve. Now that would be a story! I wanted to go over and tell the guy to meet me in the parking lot but my wife Gladys (just the kind of name this crappy writer would give her in his crappy story) told me to forget about it. That's all I have to say on the subject. Any response?

Editor: I am not sure whether you want a response concerning "true-to-life fiction" or the Dixie Truck Stop. If the former, then I generally share your concerns. Despite what reviewers for the *New York Times* may say, these are not "realistic" stories (see Nelson Goodman on this subject); further, as you suggest, the characters in this fiction are puppets and perhaps have reason to be upset at their authors (see Flann O'Brien on this subject). As to the Dixie Truck Stop, I also share your concerns about the quality of the food, and would add that the service leaves something to be desired.

Dear Editor: You be of help to me in this endeavor. Probably you have heard. I am the sole translator of the most classic Argentinean novelist, Arguoro del Postina de Parmiva Sanchez de Santa Conceiviela, also known as popularly José Farmer. You have known, certainly. I have exclusive arrangements with the distinguished brother-in-law of his former wife, a famed in her country. The novel, you know, estimated highly in all countries through the world of major integrity. Mr Farmer's story involves loves and hatreds of the Revolution of '28, you know, and the terrible turmoils of marriage betrayals in much generations of the land. I am Distinguished Visiting Professor (Adjunct) at Utah University, where I am pleased to have available office, phone, and latest technology developments for my work, that I expect completely ready for printing in 6 months, the anniversary of Mr Farmer's birthday. My beloved wife and her beloved father, my father-in-law at marriage, work all night to make this an honor for the author. My studious wife always and dedicatedly a grand help since she studied for much years in your fair country. You be pleased to see manuscript when done. We must insist on immediate publication not to offend hearts of beloved former wife and brother-in-law, so we must have produced copies and payment in 6 said months. Please make for these asute arrangements via me as being authority in charge. I have for this also a 90 page introduction which for I must insist payment now entitled "God(s) with(in) Prototypical Con(text)s: José Farmer's Life and Productions," which will draw many people to it. We respectfully will look for Dalkey Archives reply.

Editor: I am not the person you want to contact here, though I will say your project does sound intriguing and I see no reason why someone here will not jump at the opportunity to take this on. Though I am not directly involved in that part of the operation, I believe that the six-month time frame you have set is quite reasonable, though you might want to let the company know how much you require as an advance.

Dear Editor: I am rather miffed by the rather frequent attacks on the *New York Times Book Review* that show up in the pages of the *Review of Contemporary Literature*. As a regular reviewer for the *Times,* as well as a writer in my own right who has a collection of short stories forthcoming from William Morrow, I am personally offended but am also made indignant by the suggestion that people involved with the *Times* are stupid. I wouldn't claim to be the best-read person in the world, but I do believe I can tell a good novel from a bad one, one that has something to tell about the world in which we all live and one that doesn't, and one that has a good plot and one (such as the books published by Dalkey Archives) that has no plot whatsoever and seems intent on showing a reader how little he knows about the world of books and literature. And maybe you people can have a fine old life up in your ivory tower, but some of us have to worry about greasing the wheels. We all know what the deal is when we review for the *Times* and we damn well know we had better follow the rules if we expect to be asked back to do more reviews, but in general I think the reviews are fair and even insightful for the average American reader whom I think you will agree is not very bright. For instance, one of my fellow reviewers, another novelist in her own right, recently reviewed the new translation of Borges, and she rather boldly suggested that Borges has seen his day and doesn't wear too well. Now I know that this opinion is likely to aggravate you people, but I think the *Times* editors went out on a limb with this review, and I should add that the reviewer bent over backwards to be more than fair to Borges, who I find to be unreadable and boring. Rather than worrying that some people, like yourselves, would think of them as philistines and imbeciles, the editors took the risk and ran the review. If Borges had wanted his works to live beyond the little coterie of snobs that he appealed to in his lifetime, then he might have spent some time writing about what most people care about, such as divorce, farm issues, next-door neighbors, investment properties, and weddings!

Editor: The publication is called the *Review of Contemporary Fiction*, not *literature.* As to the "people" here you keep referring to, all I can tell you is that I am pretty well isolated and do not see much of them, never mind question their judgments. And I very much look forward to reading what promises to be a wonderful collection of stories.

Dear Editor: I have just become aware of something concerning myself that I find disturbing. At my recent wedding, my daughter videotaped the wonderful event. A few weeks later she brought the tape to mine and my loving husband's house to view. When I heard myself speak, I couldn't believe that it was me. What I noticed is that I used expressions over and over again, and that they are the kind of expressions that, well, you associate with old people. For instance, almost every sentence out of my mouth began with, "To tell the truth." Even when this made no sense, I still said, "To tell the truth." For instance, someone on the tape said to me that it couldn't have been a more beautiful day for the wedding, and I said, "To tell the truth, I agree, it's marvelous." Someone else said to me after the ceremony, "Well, do you feel like a married woman?" and I said, "To tell the truth, I do." What the hell sense does this make? After noticing this about myself, I started to notice that other people do this as well, and that people also have gestures or facial expressions that are along the same lines as this situation that I am describing. There was this woman in a restaurant who kept saying to people, "I'll say a prayer for you." And there was this older man who kept winking. And an older woman who kept shaking her head "no" when someone was talking to her, but then she had a friend who kept shaking her head "yes," but neither of these shakings seemed to have anything to do with what was being said. They were just habits these people had developed. Then I started noticing that I had a lot of expressions I used that were like this, but perhaps the most annoying was that I kept using the word "join," like "Can I join you for dinner?" or "May I join you on your walk?" or "I think I'll join you." My question is this: what does it mean that people use these kinds of expressions and make these gestures? How does this happen?

Editor: Well, a great deal of research has been done on this subject, primarily focused on the fact that children don't behave this way but that adults do. A recent study by Johns Hopkins University scientists suggests that people's brains have only so much room for absorbing new ways of relating to the world around them, and thus develop expressions or manners of behavior that serve as reactions to most things, regardless of the apparent content. They discovered that people, aside from child actors, begin to develop these mechanisms around the age of 16, and that they frequently begin to occur as these teenagers interact with children. It's strange that you mention a wedding because many of these expressions relate to things people say at weddings, as well as funerals. Frequently, teenagers will start to use these expressions as a way of ridiculing adults, but at some point they quietly slip into using the same vocabulary.

Dear Editor: I wrote a review of one of your novels for *Publishers Weekly,* but as you can imagine I have to pull a few punches there because you never know whose toes you might be stepping on. I really didn't like the book at all but I had to say a few nice things.

When the review got published, it made me look stupid, like I couldn't make up my mind about whether it was any good or not. To make a long story short, the book is Peter Dimock's *A Short Rhetoric for Leaving the Family,* which to my mind is pretty lousy, though I realize that other people may have different opinions. I think it's lousy because the narrator-character is really a jerk and I didn't have any sympathy for him, which is the least I think an author can do for the reader. Another thing is that he repeats a lot of stuff in the book and I found the repetition rather tiresome. Why does he have to repeat things? I wish that he would have taken up the space telling us new things, like maybe explaining a few things that aren't too well explained. But instead of explaining anything, he just repeats himself more than is necessary in my opinion. And to tell the truth, this whole business about rhetoric is confusing to me. Who the hell cares about rhetoric? He seems to quote from Cicero and maybe others, but who has the time these days to look up such things? And finally, in a novel (if you will excuse the expression) about Vietnam, why don't we find out more about what really happened there such as what we do in other real novels about this tragic war?

Editor: I will tell you people once again that Dalkey Archive Press is, apparently, a separate operation from the *Review of Contemporary Fiction.* I don't know the people there and have no idea why they publish what they do. I have read this book, however, and agree that there is a fair amount of repetition. As to why he doesn't tell you more about Vietnam, all that I can guess is that he figured this information was available elsewhere. I really don't know.

Dear Editor: My husband (I will call him "Stu") and I moved to a nice little small town a few years ago to escape the downright unfriendliness of the big city. We found the perfect little house in a lovely neighborhood, a Cape Cod that would make you feel you were living in New England. At first, everything was fine. We would wave to the neighbors and they would wave back, just what you would expect in small-town America. But we didn't seem to be making any friends. So, I just rolled up my sleeves and started baking like crazy: banana bread, chocolate chip cookies, good old-fashioned American white bread hot and toasty from the oven, and all kinds of other homemade things. Did I keep them for me and "Stu"? You bet not. I would bring them to the neighbors, ring their doorbell, and give them a good old neighborly greeting. I started doing this on almost a daily basis, but still we weren't making friends, like the kind you go and have coffee with in their kitchens while the kids are out playing or the kind you talk to over the fence until the cows come home. After a while, they stopped coming to the doors when I would bring my homemade baked goods, even though I kind of thought they were in there. In the meantime, they would have their Halloween parties and their Christmas parties and their July 4th parties, the type of parties where everybody is invited. But we weren't invited. I even got to the point where I would turn off all of our lights so that they would think we weren't home and that we were probably enjoying ourselves with friends. Last summer there was even a block party, but once more we were not invited to their damn party. I could see from behind our early American curtains that there were people at this party whom weren't even from our block! Then over a week ago, some of my delicious baked goods started winding up on our front step. At seven in the morning, when "Stu" gets up for the day to get the paper, he came in with three loaves of plum bread that I had brought around to neighbors the day before. The next day he brought in four trays of pecan cookies that were freshly baked and distributed the day before. Well, this went on for several days. Three nights ago there was a heavy downpour, it just seemed to rain cats and dogs all night long. When "Stu" opened the door, it looked like a big pile of dog shit! The day before I had made nut-'n-fudge brownies for everyone and they had deposited them right there in the rain at our front door. As usual, "Stu" didn't say anything, just kind of threw the big mess into the sink and gave me one of his looks. I said to him, "Well you had better clean up that mess before our daughter Gladys comes down for the day!" He just kept right on reading that paper like he had gone deaf and couldn't hear a word I was saying. I tried to explain to him once again that some people are just a bit hard to warm up to and I was sure that if we just gave them some time, we would have friends before you could say Jimmy Cricket. The next morning, when "Stu" opened the door to get his damn old newspaper, there were my chocolate delight cookies smeared against our door. "Stu" just got his coffee and sat down to read the paper, just a smidgen crankier than usual. But later that day I found him in the TV room, which we had decorated to look like a George Washington type room, stone dead. He had blown his brains out. Just a tiny hole in his forehead, but a hole in the back big enough to drive a milk truck through! Well, I've about reached the end of my rope with the neighbors. I think their unfriendliness just finally got to old "Stu" and he gave up trying to make friends. I am just sitting and staring at the pile of delicious hickory bread that I made this morning but just don't think our neighbors deserve any. Today at the funeral, not a single one of them came to pay their respects to "Stu." Neither Gladys nor I know how to drive and so I don't know how I would even get all these loaves up and down all of these blocks. When I asked Gladys if she would help, she just said,

"Fuck 'em," like she was raised like some kind of truck driver to speak that way. I wanted to wash her mouth out, but I suppose she was just grieving for her dead Dad. Should I give them another chance? What's wrong?

Editor: I say yes, go on giving them more chances. You just never know when people will change. I think that they may have been too busy to respond to you, and as far as I can tell, you never even introduced yourself or gave them your name. The fact that they returned your baked goods to you is, I think, merely a sign that they felt guilty and that this was their way of letting you know that they were thinking of you.

Dear Editor: What's with Peter Dimock's *Rhetoric for a Family?* This was a very depressing book, I thought, and the author missed several opportunities to make it the kind of novel that a reader would find uplifting. If I had written the novel, I would have made the narrator-hero a man who is looking back on his life and his Vietnam experience. He would be a man who was injured in the war, perhaps having lost a leg or arm or both. At first he's very angry about this turn of events, but then we begin to see him mellowing, almost as though the missing appendages have made him a better man and opened him up to other people and their suffering, whereas up to this point he was merely concerned about himself and his troubles getting around the hospital ward with almost no limbs, not to mention the severe burns that have completely disfigured his face (if made into a movie, I would downplay the disfigurement bit for obvious reasons). But while in the ward he meets a beautiful young nurse who looks the world like Sandra Bullock. You might wonder how I would convince the reader that Sandra would fall for a guy who looks like he was put through a meat grinder. Well, the fact is that Sandra is blind, herself having suffered some awful trauma when young, but fortunately not something that affected her facial features. As the story moves on, we find out that our narrator-hero went on to have a very productive life, perhaps some job in Washington where he persuades hard-nosed Republicans, who turn out to have a real sentimental side to them, to start some kind of vet program and perhaps even gets some slime ball like Trent Lott sent to prison for taking kickbacks. In other words, he learns to take all of his anger about Vietnam, as well as some bitter memories about his father who always told him that he would never amount to anything, and becomes a productive—and wealthy!—citizen who gets to hump Sandra Bullock every night of the week. And out of this humping comes beautiful children who happily prance around their fifteen-room house out in some hilly section of Massachusetts, though this creates a little problem about how he gets back and forth to Washington every day, especially given the fact that he has no limbs to speak of. This is the book that I wish Peter Dimock had written rather than one that centers itself on characters who are not likable and who do not wind up humping Sandra Bullock. At the end of *my* novel, you would be glad to be an American and would also have a somewhat positive feeling about war (e.g., that it makes you a man, settles unresolved issues with your father, and gets you money and Sandra). I don't know why Mr. Dimock didn't write the novel I have outlined here rather than the grim one he did.

Editor: I don't know either. As I am sure you know, no blockbuster movies are let loose on an unsuspecting public until they have been audience tested, at which time the endings may be changed if the audience has a bad reaction. Perhaps publishers should try the same thing. By the way, the novel is called *A Short Rhetoric for Leaving the Family.*

Dear Editor: I once tried reading a novel called *The Sky Is Changing* by Gilbert Sorrento and the damn thing nearly made me puke. It reminded me of my own unhappy marriage and the last thing I needed was to have my face rubbed in it by this supposed novel. Where in the hell does a guy come up with ideas for such things and why does he think anyone would want to get depressed by reading it? This has to be the most depressing thing anyone has ever heard of. After about fifty pages of the book, I stopped reading and turned on the television. As a matter of fact, I haven't tried reading a novel since then. My marriage still stinks but at least I don't have to read about it in a book like this anymore. And besides, television can give you a few laughs, unlike this novel.

Editor: I believe the novel you are referring to is *The Sky Changes* by Gilbert Sorrentino. Yes, you are right, it is a very depressing novel and should be required reading for all of those who are about to enter the state of marriage. But once you are married, there is no point in reading the book because, as you indicate, it will only depress you.

Dear Editor: I just finished reading Peter Dimock's *Rhetoric for a Short Family*. The thing that bothered me is that the main character is not very sympathetic. Or if you will excuse my French, he is a real son of a bitch. Why couldn't the author make him more sympathetic? Who wants to read a book about someone they don't like? What's the point? Can I get my money back?

Editor: I don't really have answers to your questions. Again, the title of the novel is *A Short Rhetoric for Leaving the Family.*

Dear Editor: I've gotten myself into a hell of a mess and I hope you can help. My wife left me years ago and then I lived alone, except for my three kids, who lived with me. They of course drove me nuts and so I moved into the basement, got my own telephone line, got a dog, and just kind of took it easy for years. Except for my job, of course, which kept me busy, except when I would get "hurt." You see, I was in the handyman business, and would arrange to have an accident every once in a while and then sue the poor bastard. So, I had a pretty good life, if at times lonely. Just me and my *Playboys* for a long time, except for the occasional dating, but you know how that is, women in their thirties or forties who have been around the block several times. Nothing you would want to show off to friends. And then I had my hunting, which has always been my favorite sport and would give me the opportunity for some exercise and getting out into nature. There's a place I would go to in Wisconsin where they would let loose a few dozen birds and I'd just sit back and blow their fucking heads off. But even this got boring after a while. So, there I was, pretty much alone, and then the kids were grown up and gone, though I'm not sure where in the hell they went to. All I know is that I didn't hear the goddamn racket anymore upstairs. They got married or something, the way kids do. Then the surprise of my life hit. There was this woman living next door that I always kind of had a thing for, but the closest I could get to her was to fix things in her house, as I told you I was in the handyman business. Well, one day I'm talking to her and guess what? She's getting a divorce! The guy she was married to was some arrogant son of a bitch who I think always looked down on me because of my profession and the fact that I never finished high school. Well, one thing led to another, and before the guy was out the door, I'm in her bed, or she's in mine! Everything's going great, though of course she plays that game of "I'm not ready for this and that," the way divorcing women do. You know, she just kind of held back a lot, especially in bed, and there I was pent up like a dam about to burst after all of those years of *Playboys*. Well, more things led to other things, and we sorta move into together and then make the announcement to her kids, who are real pains in the ass, and one of them was still kind of living with her, though she shipped him off to some drug rehabilitation place pretty damn quick, though this created problems about whether her ex was still going to pay the bills. Before I know it, I'm writing checks to her and paying a lot of her bills. Well, things go on, I sell my house and move into hers and she starts in with big dreams of building a mansion. That's fine, except I'm the one supposedly coming up with all of the money because she hasn't sold her house yet. We build the fucking mansion and she finally sells her house after I work my ass off fixing it up because I am in this handyman kind of business. We move into our mansion. I bring up the subject of her part of the expenses and the money she got from selling her house, and then she announces that this is "her" money, not ours. So, on we go. The wedding plans begin, and she had BIG PLANS. It was like she wanted to invite anyone she had ever met, including her ex's family and friends! $30,000 more out the window. And $5,000 for her white wedding dress, like she had never been through this before. And of course I am the one paying for all of this, though the money for the wedding dress was, she said, a "loan." Well, the ex's family shows up at this fucking thing and I feel like they are giving me the fish-eye, you know, next-door neighbors and now we are getting married and you can tell they are standing there wondering how long this thing was going on before the divorce. And of course I kind of knew them from before, when I was just the neighbor, the "fix-it guy." And then all of her family was there. Her mother and her father are both in their eighties and they want nothing to do with me. I'm just some dumb Italian handyman unfit for their daughter. In fact, before the marriage they invited us to their house only once. The old man stayed upstairs the whole time and the mother kept looking at me like I should be outside washing their car or fixing their roof. And she kept saying things to me like, "You probably wouldn't understand since your Italian." And one time she told me not to touch the tablecloth because I would get grease on it. And my wife to be just goes along with all of this, like she's standing there thinking I'm just a dumb Italian too. And the rest of her family treats me like shit too. She's got this one sister whose married to a guy who had an elevator fall on his head. Can you believe this? It sounds like a joke, but it's true. And the last thing you want is to try to have a conversation with him. He like goes into a trance and just keeps talking. Unless there's a television around and then he goes into a trance watching television. But even this guy kind of treats me like I'm some kind of greasy Italian workman, like I should be mending shoes. And I don't even want to get into the rest of her family or I'll be here all day. So, I am beginning to think I have been taken for a ride. I'm out thousands and thousands of dollars and the bills keep rolling in. In fact, I've even started getting notices from my bank about bounced checks that my wife has written, which then leads to a big argument about money and she starts telling me that I am being abusive because I don't believe her bullshit story about the bank making all of these mistakes. And last night I got calls from Lord & Taylor and Marshall Field's about late payments and cutting off my credit. I didn't even have credit cards with these places before I got married to this woman! So, of course, there was a hell of a fight last night too, and I'm supposed to believe that these stores are also making mistakes.

Now I want to make clear that I really love this woman and she treats me really well, especially if I get sick. I mean, if I'm sick, she's always in our bedroom making the bed and vacuuming and dusting and turning the lights on and opening blinds and trying to make things cheerful for me. So, she's a very considerate person and I am very attracted to her, as I was when she was just the neighbor. And I also feel sorry for her because of what her first husband put her through, and her mother is an old drunk, and to escape her husband's mistreatment she had to have a number of affairs when she was married, which she found very disgusting. The only real complaint I have about her is that she won't let me subscribe to *Playboy* anymore because she thinks this is inappropriate ("inappropriate" is her favorite word, by the way). But I am beginning to think that the money is going to run out someday, or at least that *my* money will. I feel guilty saying all of these things and maybe I should just appreciate her for who she is, which is what her therapist tells her I should do. What do you think?

Editor: Oh, I think you should just appreciate her. But I was wondering about your treatment when ill. Do you like having the vacuum cleaner running next to you?

Dear Editor: Despite what has been said and written, and despite a few mistakes in the twentieth century, aren't Germans human too?

Editor: Apparently not. Most recent studies on this subject generally agree that the German people are more a symbol of evil than they are real people. One researcher at the Cornell Medical Center has stated in his article "Germans: People or Not?": "People? I think not. Do people do what the Germans have done?" Yet a biologist at Loras College in Dubuque, Iowa, has claimed that they "may well be human," but of a very low order, a part of the race that "psychologically never developed beyond the Stone Age." As might be expected, however, a researcher at the "Institute" in Hamburg, Germany, has written in his article "More than Human": "We are merely misunderstood." So, while there are disagreements among the experts, let's just say that most of them are highly doubtful about the human status of Germans.

Dear Editor: I am a happily married person who is having trouble with his wife with whom I have been married to for about twenty years. I don't know how to explain this well but she seems to live in a kind of fantasy world. One example of this is that she has this huge collection of miniatures, most of which she makes herself. One example of this is that she keeps making dollhouses, and then makes all of the furniture and decorations and people who live in them. After that she makes these beautiful gardens for them, and at

Christmas she turns them into the perfect Christmas houses, and even has a miniature fireplace in them. And she also tried to make our own home like these miniatures. It's like our lives are an imitation of these fantasies she has, or that she gets from women's magazines, or wherever the hell she comes up with them. One example of this is that at Christmas time she dresses the same way that she has the people in her dollhouses dress, and sometimes she starts talking about these people in the dollhouses as though they are her friends and relatives. She will actually say things like, "Martha is visiting with the children for the holidays." But we don't know anyone named Martha! I put up with these things gladly for many years, but she is only getting worse as the years go on. Sometimes I will mention someone in our real life and she won't know who I am referring to, like if they aren't from her dollhouse world, then they don't exist. She has also started writing the life histories of her dollhouse friends in these tiny little books she has. They aren't really books, though. They are these miniature books, and so of course you can't really read what she writes in them. But she will say things to me like, "Oh, my dear, I read today that this is the fifth anniversary of Cousin Alberta's death." She actually has made up histories for these people! All of this wouldn't be a problem except that we have two teenage kids who are kind of out there on the edge of things. You know, drugs and booze and sleeping around, but my wife is just completely out of it. One night my daughter was sticking her ass out the window and my wife didn't even seem to care. I should say that, in case you are wondering, I don't know why my daughter was sticking her ass out the window, but I am not in a good position to make judgments about such things because, ever since my accident a long time ago, I too have done some pretty strange things, many of them related to girls' underwear, I am ashamed to admit. Also as a result of my accident, I developed a strange habit of remembering verbatim things that I read even though I can't make any sense of them. This habit strikes people as making me seem very intelligent until they kind of catch on to the fact that I am just sort of rambling and rambling. One example of this is that I read various encyclopedias and I remember everything I read exactly, and then some night at a party some guy will refer to something that I have read, and then I launch into this really long thing where I recite the whole encyclopedia entry word for word. One example of this is that if someone says something about diesel fuel and regular gasoline, I'm off to the races. I can't control myself. Depending upon how long the entry was, I might go on for a whole hour. When I stop, I notice that the guy has usually gone away and I am just talking to myself, and I haven't understood a word I said.

You might imagine that people try to avoid me at these social gatherings, and over the years I have begun to feel like a freak. Once I got out of the elevator business, I became a gardening engineer, and that's what I am today, with a few bumps along the way, such as going bankrupt a few times, before I started to work for someone else cutting lawns and putting in bushes. Sometimes I think my wife is ashamed of what I do and this may be why she has her fantasy world. She, by the way, is the one who calls me a gardening engineer. That's how she introduces me to people and that's how she refers to me to her dollhouse friends and family. I can't quite remember what I wanted to ask you about. I'll just end by saying that my wife's family are really a bunch of nuts. Her father weighs about a thousand pounds and sits around doing nothing all day. And her mother is a big drunk who, like most alcoholics, is always going on candy binges, especially with Snicker bars, which they try to hide from their guests. Everyone else in her family is nuts too. She has one sister who ran away with some immigrant who was her next-door neighbor. I tried to help her a lot in her divorce but she wound up getting pissed off all of the time. Then she has this other sister that I kind of had a thing for and used to make obscene phone calls to. I am not proud of this behavior, but as I say, the accident did strange things to me. And the rest of them are queers and drug addicts and things like that. And they are also a very religious family and are always talking about miracles and things that Catholics believe in. One example of this is that if someone dies, they all claim that they got a message from the person, like a rosebush bloomed in the middle of winter, or water starts pouring out of some picture they have of the person, or the person visits them in a dream and tells them something about their lives. All kind of weird stuff like that. I guess that my point here is that our house is getting overrun with all of these miniature things and I hardly have any room. Should I try to get a reconstruction loan and build another room onto the house?

Editor: Yes.

Dear Editor: My screwball parents decided to move from Chicago to some crummy little town down in what's called "Central Illinois," which means the middle of nowhere. I of course was not happy about this. Back in Chicago my mother was a nurse, and you know the kind of people who go into that profession. I'm not sure what in the hell my father did, but he apparently retired when we moved to this place. Well, my mother really flipped out once we got here. She started calling me by the wrong name and began turning our house into Martha Stewart's worst nightmare. She would take any piece of old crap and try to make it a decoration of some kind. One of her things for a while was cutting out dumb pictures from magazines and putting them on a piece of wood and then shellacking them. You should have seen the junk she came out with, and then she would get all excited and ask me if I didn't think they were just the prettiest pieces of art I had ever seen in my whole life. If I told her that they were junk, she would start to cry; if I told her that they were beautiful, then I knew she would just make more of them and keep bugging me. I don't know what my father thought about all of this. He just seemed to watch television a lot or something. Just to get away from both of them as much as I could, I got a job at a restaurant on the edge of town, which is really a joke thinking that this town can have an edge. I mean the whole fucking place is just an edge. A lot of truck drivers come in there and they of course pay a lot of attention to me. Even though I am only fifteen, I started having sex with a lot of them in their rigs, something I am not too proud of, but what in the hell was I supposed to do? If I went home to good old Mom and dad, then I would have to look at all of that crap that Mom was making, or even worse she would try to make me eat all kinds of shit that she was baking for the neighbors. If you ever tasted Mom's cooking, you would know that you would rather eat her so-called "art work" than her cookies or pies or cake or bread. Last week, after dad died, she baked a pear pie. Can you imagine what this was like? Who in the hell ever heard of a pear pie? But she was all excited and said that the mourners from the funeral would love it. But there weren't any mourners. Just me and Mom, which made me late for work, something that bugged the hell out of me. After we got home from the so-called funeral without any mourners, she threw the fucking pear pie at the wall and started swearing, the way she used to do before we moved from Chicago. I told her that Martha Stewart wouldn't like that, and then she really went nuts. Now she is talking about moving to an even smaller town. What am I supposed to do? All of my friends are here, even though most of them are the truckers I mentioned before. I know that if I go on humping all of them, I'll just turn out to be a slut, but I am not about to have to make new friends in some other fucking town. I really love my Mother and don't want to hurt her, but I think I should have a life too. I asked one of my friends at the truck stop what I should do, but he just grabbed my ass, the way he always does, and then we went out to his rig, and so he wasn't too much help, and besides he is about as old as my father was before my father died in his accident. What should I do?

Editor: Your dilemma is not a uncommon one. You want your independence and your mother wants you to stay close to her. I think that you need to open up the lines of communication with your mother and share your feelings. Share your trucker experiences with her, and also be honest about what you think of her art and her food. She will appreciate this honesty and the two of you can move on to a better, more mature kind of relationship.

Dear Editor: Do you think the dead remain with us?

Editor: Yes they do, always.

Book Reviews

Guy Davenport. *Objects on a Table*. Counterpoint, 1998. 116 pp. $27.00.

Apples and pears, napkins, flowers, busts, bottles of wine—landscapes on a table, as it were—commonly make up the genre of the "still life." For certain artists (Chardin and Braque come to mind), such silent objects became the subject of their major forms of expression. Polymath Guy Davenport's wonderfully eclectic book is composed of a series of four meditations explaining why and how painters have employed this form to such vital effect. Finding patterns, he supports his observations with hundreds of wayward facts and original thoughts and superb cultural insights.

Davenport believes that "an utterly primitive and archaic feeling that a picture of food has some sustenance" is "the real root of still life." Permutations of food pictures, pheasants to peaches to plates to pots, have come down to us from prehistoric times. "Reiteration," observes Davenport (always a scholar), "is a privilege of still life denied many other modes."

Literature plays a strong role in these essays. In "The Head as Fate" we are given a brief explanation of the human bust, mostly by way of Poe, as a feature of his subject. Heads—Nefertiti's, Caesar's, Beethoven's, Pallas Athena's—described as "mankind's fateful symbol," come into the category. (The House of Usher is of course allegorically a head to a degree, Davenport isn't the first to point out.) Davenport sees Keats as fascinated with the motif, along with the likes of Milton, Shelley, and James Joyce. ("The first sentence of *Ulysses* is one: 'Stately, plump Buck Mulligan came from the stairhead, bearing a bowl of lather on which a mirror and a razor lay crossed.' ") This motif preoccupied Pouissin, Monet, and van Gogh. Picasso painted apples ("the fall") and pears ("redemption") for seventy-five years. *Objects on a Table* is a tidy journal of visual moments memorializing the treatment. As usual, Davenport's erudition, finding still lifes in unlikely places, is a singular joy. Exactitude and his taste for the kind of outré facts which delights Davenportians like myself, observations on everyone from Xenophanes, Umberto Eco, Charcot, Theocritus, and DeChirico to Nietzsche, William Carlos Williams, and Conan Doyle, are only part of the bouquet Davenport lays on our table. [Alexander Theroux]

Yoel Hoffmann. *Bernhard*. Trans. Alan Treister with Eddie Levenston. New Directions, 1998. 172 pp. $22.95.

The most immediately striking feature of this novel, the second available to us in English from the wonderful Romanian-born Israeli writer Yoel Hoffmann, is its unique structure. Covering an eight-year period from 1938 to 1946, the book is divided into 172 short sections, the majority of which are contained within a single page. Each section ends with a phrase that, repeated, opens the following section. The story, set primarily in Jerusalem, revolves around Bernhard Stein, who has become a widower just prior to the beginning of the novel. Even at the novel's close, as he writes about his wife's death to her sister, Bernhard is grieving.

During the years of the war (while Hitler invades Poland, Rommel is defeated in Egypt, and the U.S. drops bombs on Hiroshima and Nagasaki), Bernhard grieves, conjures up his past life in Berlin, talks with his friend Gustav, and constructs fictional characters who roughly parallel the central players in his own life. The minutiae of daily personal life are juxtaposed with historical events: "In January, the Red Army captures Auschwitz. Water freezes in the pipes [in Jerusalem]. Gustav boils water in a kettle and pours it on the pipes, and a white mist rises and spreads in the air of the room."

In some odd way this novel might be considered a myth of national origins, a story of modern Israel in its fetal state. The connection between the Holocaust and the establishment of Israel is implied. The mood here is hardly jubilant; rather, Bernhard seems to trudge about in a state of numbness and sorrow. An uncanny calm belies, masks, or denies underlying conflicts and tensions associated with the legitimacy of territorial claims. The very (postmodern) form of the novel allows the silences to have a powerful presence. The words are as sparse as stones in a desert: a stark dialogue between the said and the unsaid. [Allen Hibbard]

———————

Christine Brooke-Rose. *Next.* Carcanet, 1998. 210 pp. £9.95.

Having apparently said farewell to literature in *Textermination* (1991) and written her memoirs in *Remake* (1996), Brooke-Rose surprises us with a new novel as strong as anything she has ever written. Here she largely leaves behind the mediascape of her "Intercom Quartet" of the eighties and early nineties and ventures out into the streets to imagine the inner lives and outer wanderings of London's homeless. It's hard to picture Brooke-Rose sleeping rough at seventy-five years old or even interviewing those who do, but however she conducted her research, the result is as plausible and freshly observed as if firsthand.

This being a Brooke-Rose novel, there are structural secrets, some of which are revealed by the jacket copy; for instance, there are twenty-six characters, each bearing a name beginning with a different letter of the alphabet, the ten homeless characters spelling out among them the ten letters of the top row of the keyboard (QWERTYUIOP). This time around, however, the Oulipian cryptograms and procedures seem less crucial than a couple of features that the text displays on its surface. One element is the book's mapping of street-level, fin-de-millennium London, as we track the homeless on their rounds from doorway doss to homeless shelter to job center and around again, placing *Next* firmly in the lineage of the great twentieth-century city novels—a London "Wandering Rocks" for the nineties. More extraordinary still is Brooke-Rose's registration of the varieties of London speech (or "Estuarian," as she calls it), ranging from educated bureaucratese through mildly "flavored" standard to immigrant variants to the pure, uncut thing itself: "Shi', Olley, wey can't tauwk in this craowd. We'uw loowse each ather anywie. Auw yer neeyd is ter skidadduw." This language is a great discovery, or invention, or whatever it is, and puzzling it out is not only one of the superior pleasures of this text but something like an exercise in sympathy and identification; in struggling to voice this notation, you find yourself imaginatively occupying the space of those whose speech it simulates.

It turns out that you *can* teach an old lady (as she calls herself in *Remake*) new tricks; or, more to the point, she can teach them to you. [Brian McHale]

Barbara Croft. *Necessary Fictions*. Univ. of Pittsburgh Press, 1998. 224 pp. $22.50.

In the visually acute and psychologically perceptive stories collected in *Necessary Fictions,* Barbara Croft fixes her characters at the junctures where loss and art intersect. These characters, many of them artists and writers whose careers have stalled, turn their techniques to their personal lives. The situations that result seem like setups for elaborate jokes about the creative proclivities of writers and artists, although the punch line always seems tragic rather than funny: the writer protagonist in "The Woman in the Headlights," who can't shake his depression two years after a car accident in which he struck and killed a pedestrian, uses his skills for invention to create a new life for himself; the artist in "Three Weeks in Italy and France," who, though she hasn't been painting, tackles her garden with a sharp eye toward color and form. Constructed with an eye toward the parallels between art and life, Croft's stories are filled with carefully wrought images which are extensions of her themes. Though clearly the work of a writer assured and knowledgeable in her craft, the deliberately artistic images often seem self-conscious and draw attention away from the situations and characters, which Croft has so compellingly created.

In the second section of her book, a novella and three interconnected short stories which map the life of the Gerhardt family, Croft's gifts are on full display. The occasion of the sale of her childhood home provides Maggie Gerhardt, the family's self-appointed historian, with the opportunity to revisit emblematic family moments—their search for the perfect, American-Dream house, the truth behind her father's death, her brother's actions in Vietnam. As Maggie puzzles through her family's history, the images and family stories repeat, and the narrative flashes forward and back until, remarkably, the snaking threads of the stories combine to produce a narrative akin to the fabric of memory. In reckoning the hopes of the Gerhardts' past with the disappointment that has bloomed for them in the present, Croft demonstrates the force and veracity behind *Necessary Fictions;* recounting stories is as vital to the present as it is to retaining the past. [Nicole Lamy]

Patti Smith. *Patti Smith Complete: Lyrics, Reflections & Notes for the Future*. Doubleday, 1998. 246 pp. $35.00.

"The first song I remember singing is 'Jesus Loves Me.' I can picture myself singing it while sitting on a stoop in Chicago, waiting for the organ grinder to come up the street with his pet monkey," writes the Queen of Punk Rock in an unadorned two-page preface to this collection which then moves chronologically right into songs from her *Horses* LP and "Gloria," with her pretentious but romantic announcement, "Jesus dies for somebody's sins, but not mine," all of it giving us the theological bookends that hold her sacred/profane presentations. "Use menace, use prayer," she quotes Jean Genet in the "Easter" section of the book. I love Patti Smith. She believes in herself, hates authority, is strong. She's a tall dark winged angel of confusion, daring, a lot of a kind of genius, womanly courage, and beauty. She is capable of a razor of a line, almost always simple:

> In the medieval night
> 'Twas love's design
> And the sky was open
> Like a valentine
> All the lacy lights
> Where wishes fall
> And like Shakespeare's child
> I wished on them all.

Shakespeare's child, Rimbaud's avatar, Ginsberg's friend, Burroughs's buddy—and there are photos of Hendrix, Joan of Arc, Bob Dylan, Pope John Paul I, Kurt Cobain, Jackie Onassis all through the book—Patti worships heroes, paradigms mostly who embody various sides of herself: the sexy, defiant, poetic, rude, ass-kicking rocker of "Piss Factory," "Because the Night," "People Have the Power," and an anthem of the sixties that she just happened to write in 1988. Her lyrics are simple and spare, allusive, narrative, drumbeating:

> He sings a black embrace
> And white opals swimming
> In a child's leather purse
> Have you seen death swimming
> Have you seen death swimming

and meant to be sung. I own many videos of her rocking, early and late, in Germany, France, Manhattan, being interviewed, waltzing in motion, throwing her legs, bashing her guitar, and yet what is amazing to me is her constant ability, almost mythically, to show a spiritual side to what is presented with rocking-horse urgency, angry youth, and dissatisfaction. She is a quester, asking hard questions in her music:

> It's wild wild wild wild
> Wild wild wild wild

and always coming off so much more honest than people like Burroughs and Ginsberg and Cobain and lot of other yahoos she pushes. She is a waif and a street girl, has had her difficulties, fallen off stage, lost her husband, Fred "Sonic" Smith of MC5, as well as her brother Todd and close friend Robert Mapplethorpe. Maybe because she so completely dropped out once before, for decades, going to Detroit to get married, have two kids, raise them, and be a mother, I am convinced that she's the kind of person who would go to a convent or live in a desert to pray or become a true anchorite or just disappear, in a good way, getting rid of the world she knows is dumb.

> I was feeling sensations in no dictionary
> He was less than a breath of shimmer and smoke
> The life in his fingers unwound my existence
> Dead to the world alive I awoke.

Patti Smith doesn't need the world in ways that a lot of common people do. The thing about her, for all the wildness at CBGB and flip profanity and photos in urinals and bedraggled dark shots of her wailing, these songs are prayers. All songs are, to a degree.

> I've got seven ways of going seven wheres to be
> Seven sweet disguises, seven ways of serving Thee.

But read these. They are psalms of a sort. It's true. These are prayers. Laments. Chants. Litanies. And incantations. I'm not trying to baptize the girl. But Patti Smith is a very serious woman. [Alexander Theroux]

Karen Elizabeth Gordon. *Out of the Loud Hound of Darkness: A Dictionarrative.* Pantheon, 1998. 210 pp. $23.00.

For fifteen years now, Karen Elizabeth Gordon has been publishing grammar and usage handbooks with a difference. Instead of old tired phrases from equally old and tired grammarians, she offers what she calls a "Balkanalian tour of Babel" (xiii), complete with (1) a cast of reappearing and quite strange characters (carefully described in the *Dramatis Personae* section at the book's beginning), (2) recurring narrative threads (used to piece together a series of stories), (3) a plethora of strange and mildly bizarre images, and (4) sentences that have the mood of a Mervyn Peake novel.

Take, for instance, one of the sentences used to illustrate the difference between *eremetic* and *hermetic:* "King Alabastro kept Dariushka's eyeballs and heart in a hermetically sealed bivalve coffer, her garter belt entwined with his suspenders, her finger cymbals with his cuff links, and her slingback satin slippers at the foot of their conjugal bed." Or this sentence, which distinguishes between *fray* and *affray:* "The affray at Blotto Junction could have followed a much bloodier scenario had Ziggie Spurthrast not appeared in her leopard-skin getup and shot down a row of whiskey bottles

. . . ." Not exactly the world of Dick and Jane.

There are one or two slips (for instance, *The Drunken Boat* is attributed to Baudelaire rather than Rimbaud—though perhaps this is the fault of Drat Siltlow, the character who tells us this, rather than of Gordon), but the usage rules are all carefully and effectively drawn. Gordon manages to transform a dry art into a rollicking one, creating a fragmented dark universe at the same time. There's no more delightful way to approach usage and grammar than through the work of Karen Elizabeth Gordon. [Brian Evenson]

Albert J. Gerard. *Suspended Sentences*. John Daniel and Company, 1998. 135 pp. Paper: $12.00.

I have admired Gerard's fiction for many years; I reviewed *Christine/ Annette* and *The Hotel in the Jungle* in this periodical. I am pleased that this excellent collection of short stories is now available.

The dates of publication for the six stories range from 1933 (when Gerard was eighteen) to 1993; the stories appeared in *Hound and Horn, Story, The Magazine* (a short-lived periodical which contained work by Robert Penn Warren, R. P. Blackmur, and Caroline Gordon—one of the advisors was Yvor Winters). Although the stories are set in Davos, New York City, Mazatlán, and other "exotic" places, they share the obsessive concern with perverse marriage, of attraction and repulsion, and a "taste for risk" (to use one of the titles). They forcefully explore the "heart of darkness" we find in those writers Gerard has discussed in his criticism: Conrad, Faulkner, Gide, and Dostoyevsky.

Perhaps the two best stories are "Miss Prindle's Lover" and "The Incubus." They are dark meditations on the sickness of love (or vice versa); they give us tangled motives, Gothic shudders. The protagonists try to be "safe" but they find that they are bewitched. The women they love are sinister—even if they don't mean to be—and they overwhelm innocent, structured lives. Gerard recognizes that in the affairs there is a complicated bond of lover and beloved, victim and victimizer—a bond which is expressed in wonderful language.

Look closely at this passage: "Miss Prindle had stopped speaking, and now, as I stood by the window, I felt utterly alone. A friendly voice had ceased, and the room was filled with foreign sounds. I thought of her as an insane and disgusting woman." The clarity of the style heightens the nightmarish affair—and makes us question the narrator's vision. Isn't he disgusting in his rush to judgment? Isn't he "foreign"? And once we question his sentences, we are compelled to suspend quick evaluation.

Gerard is an admirable writer because he gives us this "life of nerves." And he implicates us; he makes us secret sharers. [Irving Malin]

Knut Hamsun. *Under the Autumn Star*. Trans. Oliver and Gunnvor Stallybrass. Sun & Moon Press, 1998. 112 pp. $11.95.

This reprint will be welcomed by admirers of Knut Hamsun (1859-1952), the Norwegian Nobel Laureate of 1920 who influenced several major American novelists, including Ernest Hemingway, Henry Miller, and Paul Auster. Another follower, Isaac Bashevis Singer, went so far as to say that the whole modern school of fiction in the twentieth century stems from Hamsun.
　　Originally published in 1906, *Under the Autumn Star* is a comic novel narrated by an itinerant worker, Knut Pedersen. Set in a rural landscape and written in a technically conventional mode, the book lacks the halluci-natory fervor and intensity of Hamsun's finest work, including the early masterpiece *Hunger* (1890), an alienated ramble through Christiania (now Oslo), which arguably marks the birth of the modernist ethos. Compared with the urban outcast who narrates *Hunger*, the scapegrace Pedersen and his cohorts in *Under the Autumn Star* bear only a distant resemblance to the spiritual exiles of, say, Henry Miller. Despite the bucolic mood, however, the characteristically wry and detached idiom Hamsun explores here con-firms his standing as one of the pioneers of twentieth-century fiction of es-trangement. The translation by Oliver and Gunnvor Stallybrass is excellent, and the publisher deserves credit for keeping this and other titles by Norway's major novelist in print. [Philip Landon]

———————

Kathe Koja. *Extremities*. Four Walls Eight Windows, 1998. 202 pp. $22.00.

Although I praised Koja's last novel, *Kink,* in a previous issue for its per-verse, spellbinding explorations of a love triangle, I must admit that I was not completely prepared for the manic beauty of these stories. They remind me of a marriage of Poe and Burroughs, a relentless pursuit of extremities of behavior—behavior which is captured in the surging currents of Koja's sentences.
　　In "Arrangement for Invisible Voices"—notice the mixture of ear and eye—the protagonist cannot escape from pig sounds as they engulf his con-sciousness. The sounds destroy whatever reason he once possessed. Now he can no longer be a husband—or even a person. I quote a passage which rep-resents the wonderful style: "It was coming from the pigs. Spitted bodies, bellies dull and glowing from the fire beneath, feet tied like victims, their eyes were alive, alive, and though their small hairy mouths moved not at all the song continued to grow, to burn as they burned. Yet it was not, and he knew this, not their own prosaic torment that they mourned, oh no some-thing large, large, some huge death celebrated in accusatory song." Note the flood of words, the oddity of adjectives, the conjunction of pain and celebra-tion. Surely these sentences are carefully constructed to examine the sup-posed division of man and beast.
　　In "The Neglected Garden"—another love story, another Gothic arrange-ment—the protagonist sees his beloved as a shadowy garden. (Koja con-

tinually undermines accepted myth; she offers a black paradise.) I can't re-
sist quoting Koja's amazing dislocations, displacements, destructions of
structure. The woman's eyes are "the eyes of someone surprised by great
pain." She is transformed into flowers: "Then on each spot where the solution had struck the foliage began not to wither but to blacken, not the color
of death but an eerily sumptuous shade, and in one instant every flower in
her mouth turned black, a fierce and luminous black and her eyes were
black too, her lips, her hands black . . . that black black tongue come crawl-
ing across the grass, and she behind it with a smile."

Koja gives me the "power of blackness." But she does more: she violates
me, seducing me into some world that holds my obsessive fears of love and
death. She offers "the secret that leads us finally to where at last and always we were always meant to be." [Irving Malin]

Emer Martin. *More Bread or I'll Appear*. Houghton Mifflin, 1999. 288 pp.
$23.00.

Emer Martin's second novel is, like her *Breakfast in Babylon* (1995), a road
novel of sorts. But whereas the first novel dwelt on the troublesome stasis
of life on the bum among the self-appointed wretched of the earth, *More
Bread or I'll Appear* is a wild goose chase. Or, seeing that the novel is a port-
manteau of contemporary Irish themes (along with much, much more),
maybe it should be called a Wild Goose chase. (The Wild Geese is the pet
name given the Catholic aristocracy who went into exile at the end of the
Williamite wars to become, in time, sources of international inspiration to
those left behind.) Three hundred years later, Emer Martin gives us the
story of Aisling, who is pursued around the world—or at least from Japan to
the Mosquito Coast—by her sister, Keelin. She's accompanied intermit-
tently by an assortment of dilapidated siblings, whose stories intersect
with, overlap and go against the grain of the main quest; the overall imaginative environment might be described as amphetamine-picaresque. All
concerned are bankrolled by a Manhattan-based, whiskey-priest uncle,
himself the long standing boy toy of a Jesuit gynecologist.

In Irish, *aisling* means *vision*. In this case, Aisling embodies the complete escapee: a gender-bending, multicultural, eco-fetishising, Third
Worldist. She contains multitudes. But the rest of the characters can barely
contain themselves and fall afoul of AIDS, OCD, Vegas mob justice, heroin,
etc. However, if Keelin doesn't go along with Aisling, she risks becoming
like their deranged neighbor from childhood, whose signature phrase gives
the novel its title. Narrative bustle, sweeping ambition, sensational events,
exotic locales, long on opinion, short on thought: the phrase "the shallow
pond and the finicky peacocks" proves hard to shake. [George O'Brien]

A. G. Mojtabai. *Soon*. Zoland, 1998. 190 pp. $22.00.

Although Grace Mojtabai is one of our finest writers, she has never received the critical attention she deserves. *Soon*, a collection of "Tales from Hospice," is her best book.

In her preface Mojtabai writes: "And happening to be present at a graced moment sometimes I am startled to find—*this* side of death—the old barriers rolled away, stranger towards stranger with no other strangeness than the ease of the turning." Her best stories attempt to capture in her words, the last words of the dying protagonist.

The story "Zone"—notice that she is fond of such simple one-syllable words as *soon, zone,* and *last*—is perhaps the most daring, provocative exploration of the last words of dying patients I have ever read. Mr. Straughn, a patient at the hospice, wants to record the last word he speaks before he crosses the threshold from life to death. (The sense of doors, barriers, thresholds is vividly present throughout the collection.) He refuses to accept "borrowed thoughts, *secondhand* language" (my italics). Thus he looks at funeral cards as clichés. "He wanted to record how it feels to die, what it meant to enter what he called the end zone." The story is full of reflections; Mojtabai tries to record Straughn's words. It is a commentary on commentary; it moves on two levels.

As Mr. Straughn begins to "actively die," he finds that his words become strange, that his language now includes "zweh"—for sweat?—and as "his breathing stops, stutters, starts up again," the narrator (probably Mojtabai) finds that it's impossible to understand his language. She recognizes that she is limited in her task. Her language cannot declare his dying.

But the story doesn't end with lost connections. The last sentence is wonderfully radiant: "Mr. Straughn wanted to send, wanted desperately to say—if not whole words, then at least crumbs flung backwards as he went on ahead, so we wouldn't be so lost when the time comes for us to follow, as it surely must." The sentence is almost biblical; it is full of one-syllable words—*must, want, time, comes*—which carry mysteries of meaning (or vice versa). This one story demonstrates that Mojtabai, unlike more famous explorers of language, surely understands the boundaries of fiction, and she hopes to communicate what cannot be communicated. I salute her bravery, her "acts of attention." [Irving Malin]

Leonid Dobychin. *The Town of N*. Trans. Richard C. Borden with Natalia Belova. Intro. by Richard Borden. Northwestern Univ. Press, 1998. Paper: $14.95.

The story behind the publication of *The Town of N* is almost as interesting as the novel itself. Dobychin published the book, his only novel, in 1935, then disappeared after the public denial of his work. He was found two months later, dead of an apparent suicide. How the book was published at all, during Stalin's rule, is a mystery; immediately following publication, Soviet critics attacked the book for its "formalist" style and thematic criticism of the regime. Although contemporaries such as Tynyanov and Kaverin proclaimed Dobychin an eminent author of their time, his work was nowhere to be found until this book was republished in the late 1980s, as a result of Gorbachev's glasnost.

Dobychin uses a traditional Russian device of a child narrator; however, his nameless boy does not exist in that "ideal state" of childhood. He is not living in innocence but depending on, simply, distorted information. Over a span of ten years, the boy's primary modes of learning—adults and books—are proven faulty because of his misinterpretation. His ears and eyes deceive him: he misunderstands pretty much everything the adults say and do, only to repeat their sayings and explanations inappropriately. Literature, too, offers little true insight. Among the books he misreads is *Dead Souls;* thus the "N" in the title is a place the boy dreams about, a place he imagines he will go to and be welcomed. This mistake that the narrator makes in comparing his town with Gogol's fictive "N" (a full century later) truly points out that nothing has changed with Marxist "progress." And although nothing has changed, nothing is seen clearly either. The boy's realization of this occurs in the last chapter, when he (not) coincidentally peers through another's glasses and understands that he has been mis-seeing things all along: his books, his relationships, his understanding of the world.

The young narrator has a habit of repeating exact words that adults tell him, but uses quotation marks to set them apart. Therefore, his choice of language can be confusing at times and partially indiscernable. Borden, in his introduction, clarifies that Dobychin's original text included this punctuation, alluding to children's tendency to mark adult words that way. However, this conceit causes some distraction because the narrator's own understanding seems inconsistent.

While knowing Gogol's work (or Sologub's, which is referred to several times) is not necessary to enjoy *The Town of N*, readers may miss the full effect without that background. Dobychin's book surely offers an intriguing view into a short window of time right before fifty years of heavy censorship. Unfortunately, readers may have to wait to read more Dobychin: his short stories are still only available in Russian. [Amy Havel]

Hélène Cixous, *FirstDays of the Year.* Trans. Catherine A. F. MacGillivray. Univ. of Minnesota Press. 1998. 192 pp. Paper: $16.95; *Stigmata: Escaping Texts*. Routledge, 1998. 224 pp. Paper: $19.99.

Hélène Cixous's two new texts restage and reinvent her earlier questions about women's relations to writing and the body. Described on the book jacket as an "essay-poem," *FirstDays* investigates the boundaries of both genre and gender. The book pursues her earlier injunction that women must "write the body" in her famous essay "The Laugh of the Medusa," but this text complicates the notion of "writing" through its evocation of narrative and "story." Cixous constantly invokes the usual assumptions on which "reading" depends in order to challenge them; this book, she tells us, is "the story of losing the thread and letting oneself be guided by the voice." The relationship between "author" and "character" is central here because the narrator searches for and challenges the text's ownership. Author, mother, and daughter are terms that circulate throughout the text as Cixous investigates the relation between writing and female identity. In *Stigmata*, which collects Cixous's newest essays, she explores the intersections between poetry, philosophy, and language and looks at reading as a site of knowledge: "I would like so much this unknown untorn page. Everything we read: remains." The most compelling essay in this volume, "My Algeriance, in other words: to depart not to arrive from Algeria," reads identity's fictions, documenting her own struggles to negotiate her relation to the categories "French" and "Algerian." Her poststructuralist frame unsettles our conventional questions surrounding the rubric "identity politics." Cixous's subversion of genre distinction is endlessly fascinating, and we could read her work for its lyricism, its linguistic play, alone. But at stake in both *First Days* and *Stigmata* is the complex philosophical problem of the relation between the book and the body. Each text ultimately is, as Cixous writes in *FirstDays*, "a story of escape and navigation." [Nicole Cooley]

Radmila J. Gorup and Nadezda Obradovic, eds. *The Prince of Fire: An Anthology of Contemporary Serbian Short Stories*. Foreword by Charles Simic. Univ. of Pittsburgh Press, 1998. 371 pp. Cloth: $50.00; paper: $19.95.

Thirty-five Serbian authors and as many stories can help U.S. readers to understand the other reality of Serbia's people, showing their views through realistic, metaphysical, experimental, or creative nonfiction pieces. Not afraid of fire (the title of David's story) surrounding them, they continue to create in spite of all the obstacles, writing about the past and how it affects the present ("Skull Tower," by Hadži-Tančić, is about the 1890 slaying of Serbs by Turks whose 952 skulls were built into a tower), about the changes due to war, forced emigration (Kapor, Dimić), about rejected writers (Tišma) who cannot accept "pure, eternal Slavic suffering without which the very idea of self-respect [is] inconceivable" (Bulatović). The Black Plague (Pekić) can be applied to contemporary destruction of life in the Balkans where ordinary people don't care about art but about survival, whereas artists cannot survive without their art, so they paint horror and agony in exile (Prodanović).

Milorad Pavić creates a bridge between history and postmodernism dealing with the dichotomies of hatred and love/war and peace. Olujić writes about a woman trying to survive with jealousy and rejection; Dimovska about a woman left with a child and no means of support whose husband has died in the war. We learn more truths about the Balkans where, according to Ognjenović, "the facts are known, but the real story is avoided." The nonfiction experimental piece by Albahari recalls the author's father's time at a Nazi camp in Germany. The memoir, "The Lute and Scars," by the late Danilo Kiš asserts what binds this anthology: "The duty of man—is to exit this world leaving behind him not deeds" but something of goodness—"knowledge. Every written word is a genesis." Wounds from love leave the deepest impressions in the soul. And don't let literature replace love: "Life can't be replaced by anything." [Biljana D. Obradovic]

Thorvald Steen. *Don Carlos*. Trans. James Anderson. Sun & Moon Press, 1998. 158 pp. $21.95.

This is an epistolary novel by a Norwegian author, written from the viewpoint of an Italian laborer, set in Argentina in the year 1833, and preoccupied with the ideas of an Englishman, Charles Darwin—"El Naturalista" Don Carlos, as he is called in the book. Steen's novel strikes at the heart of western cultural history by reminding us of the spiritual shock caused by evolutionary biology.

Darwin's discoveries, which destroyed creationist theories of a divine human genesis and demonstrated a natural origin of species, were a central concern in nineteenth-century literature from Tennyson to Strindberg. Contemplation of the newly secularized universe, with its blind and inescapable forces, was for nineteenth-century writers a question of philosophical self-definition: a means of mapping out human prospects in the modern world. Twentieth-century literature of alienation also has a Darwinian lineage, although the name of the great naturalist is rarely pronounced by today's literary authors. Steen is a welcome exception. His narrator is wrenched from religious faith by Darwin's scientific outlook: "I am doomed to live with my body in the absence of God."

Technically, Steen is a close disciple of his famous compatriot, Knut Hamsun, who was in his twenties when Darwin died and whose work so powerfully charts the tribulations of the individual consciousness amid the pressures of a secular world. It may be tactless to ask what Steen adds to Hamsun's innovative subjectivism, or whether the nineteenth-century spiritual crisis was more powerfully attested by nineteenth-century authors. *Don Carlos* is an austere and ambitious book which probes the roots of modern alienation. [Philip Landon]

Franz Kafka. *The Trial*. A New Translation Based on the Restored Text. Trans. Breon Mitchell. Schocken Books, 1998. 276 pp. $24.00.

We needed a new translation of *The Trial* after the text Franz Kafka's friend Max Brod salvaged from his literary remains was given a thorough scholarly overhaul and published by Malcolm Pasley in 1990. Breon Mitchell's version renders the novel in language which suggests new subtleties in the character behind the narrative voice, limning the spectral geometry of a haunted mind. Working with more of Kafka's text than previously had been available, he adds twists absent from the 1927 English version by Willa and Edwin Muir. A professor of Germanic studies at Indiana

University, Mitchell also displays enough scholarship to interest us in the state in which the unfinished manuscript of *The Trial* was left at Kafka's untimely death from tuberculosis.

Considering the controversy surrounding Max Brod's role in sequestering what his friend Kafka told him to burn, one might have expected more differences than appear in Mitchell's new version. The former chapter on Joseph K.'s conversation with Fräulein Bürstner's friend Fräulein Montag is now relegated to "Fragments," where other newly available short episodes are revealed for the first time. Still, the essential, disturbing germ stays breathlessly intact. A creeping suspicion that the world closely resembles Kafka's fable assails the lively imagination. Why does Joseph K.'s year-long tryst with the Law fail so abjectly? Kafka's justice remains impervious to inquiry.

Mitchell's effort is more accurate in certain details, prompting us to look for more religiously oriented language absent from the older translation, for example. He aims to be more faithful in spirit to what Kafka himself never finally settled. One may also distinguish a familiarly native ring to his words, colloquial in the contemporary American idiom. What is important is that this new translation be read, especially by those for whom "Kafka" is just a storied name. [Michael Pinker]

James Thurber and E. B. White. *Is Sex Necessary?: Or, Why You Feel the Way You Do.* Common Reader/Akadine, 1998. 190 pp. Paper: $11.95.

Is Sex Necessary?, despite its seemingly salacious title, is a cheerful little book. The question that Thurber and White pose to their readers is one that modern man—and I do mean man—often ponders, or at least the modern man of 1929, when *Is Sex Necessary?* was originally written. The current reprint provides a keyhole on an era when the writings of Sigmund Freud were becoming the stuff of dinner table conversation and casting a whole new and not totally welcome light on the relationship between the sexes.

This new edition, with line drawings by Thurber and an introduction written by White in 1950, is partly a parody of popular scientific writings and partly a humorous look at love and marriage. The book is written for the confused male of the time, who is confounded by modern women and how he is expected to relate to them, given what scientists and psychoanalysts say. The chapters include "The Nature of the American Male," "How to Tell Love from Passion," "The Sexual Revolution: Being a Rather Complete Survey of the Entire Sexual Scene," and "What Should Children Tell Parents?"

The males of the book are described as ordinary guys who would like to do the right thing in regard to women, but have absolutely no idea what that is. Tips are given on relationships, including the sage advice that, in writing a letter to a woman, if "you don't care *what* punctuation mark you put after 'darling,' the chances are you are in love—although you may just be uneducated, who knows?"

Although some of the humor is dated, one can see the connections to current humorists like Dave Barry and Garrison Keillor, who often seem to be confused by the world around them. *Is Sex Necessary?* is an amusing look back at what was then called "the battle of the sexes." This edition is one of a number of wonderful but often neglected books that Common Reader has brought back into print. [Sally E. Parry]

Rebecca Brown. *The Dogs: A Modern Bestiary*. City Lights, 1998. 166 pp. $10.95.

A bestiary, the jacket of Rebecca Brown's novel tells us, is "a medieval book combining descriptions of real or mythical animals with fables designed to teach a lesson." Fraught with infelicitous typographical and even grammatical errors, the novel nevertheless does fulfill its didactic purpose, as advertised. The unnamed heroine, an "innocent," lives in a dangerous world where women are the objects of brutality and aggression. Confined to a claustrophobic life of inaction, cosmic guilt, and oppression, she awakens one day to find a Doberman bitch at her door who moves in with her and quickly takes over her life. The dog, which may or may not actually exist, becomes, in a sense, her Virgil and her demon, and she must escape the confinement of her tiny apartment and her sterile and infernal existence to find renewal in the river of rebirth at the novel's end. The heroine's dark night of the soul forces her, and us the readers, to confront our own heartless hollowness and to ask how we might remedy the end of the century malaise which we confront. Her solution? We must take matters into our own hands, and, like Candide, we must work to unearth the child within; we must tend our gardens.

Brown weaves fairy tales, a morality play, medieval fable, Christian allegory, and perhaps even a bit of magical realism into her novel with, I think, uneven success. It is not always clear how this generic mélange advances the author's plan to teach the reader a lesson. Nevertheless, fans of Robert Coover and Angela Carter will find some sustenance in Rebecca Brown, and Ms. Brown's many fans, who appreciate her terse, understated, fragmentary style, will not be disappointed. [Joanne Gass]

Gordon Lish. *Arcade, or How to Write a Novel*. Four Walls Eight Windows, 1998. 175 pp. $22.00.

One of *Arcade*'s three epigraphs is from Gilles Deleuze: "In the game of becoming, the being of becoming also plays the game with itself." Gordon Lish's *Arcade* explores both becoming as well as being, by way of a wonderful carnival of language, a language that shifts from playful to potent as frequently as Lish, the author, employs uncanny syntactical shifts.

Lish, the narrator, crawls through language and its limitations to understand the world around him, starting with his remembrance of his family's annual vacation to Laurel in the Pines where Gordon, as a child, quests after "Buried Treasure" underneath the sand in the arcade game, and finishing with his recognition, as an aged author, of the quandaries associated with fiction which include, though are not limited to, readers' expectations, authorial intent, and the factual/fictional binary of "autobiographical" fiction. After ranting about the vicarious nature of readers on page eighty-five, Lish decides, "Because I Gordon am fed up to the gills," to leave the next twenty pages blank. In the end, more than forty pages are left blank, at times even losing the pagination, relying simply on a small dot beside the absent page number.

The one disappointment of the novel is the rate of acceleration. The novel moves too quickly from childhood where Lish is particularly adept at making the syntactical shifts work to his advantage. Later, and too quickly, comes bitterness, "It makes me glad I'm the last of the Lishes. They can all of them go thank their lucky stars they did not live to see the state the English language is in." Ironically, *Arcade* finally is less about How to Write a Novel than Lish's attempt to remind readers of the joys of languages particularly since it is through language that we all discover ourselves and the world in which we live.

Near the end of the novel, in a belated epigraph, Lish quotes Alphonso Lingis: "What is the imperative in things and the imperative that we have to perceive things? The imperative is nothing less than what is commonly called life." Gordon Lish should be commended; *Arcade* is Lish at his best. [Alan Tinkler]

Richard Burgin, ed. *Jorge Luis Borges: Conversations*. Univ. of Mississippi Press, 1998. 254 pp. $17.00.

Perhaps no Latin American author was interviewed more than Jorge Luis Borges, at least in the English-language press. The fact that Borges was a speaker of English, having grown up speaking English in his home, meant that he could not only handle himself easily with English-language interviewers (something that a number of Latin American writers can do) but that he was able to handle the language with virtually the same degree of nuance and sophistication of style as his interviewers, many of whom were distinguished writers, journalists, and literary critics themselves.

Burgin has provided a lovely anthology of the best of these interviews, organized chronologically. They are prefaced with a detailed chronology of Borges's life, in order to place each interview within the context of Borges's personal life and literary career. They span the years 1966 (Richard Stern) to 1985 (Amelia Barili), which, since Borges died in 1986, must be the last interview he gave in English.

The only defect of the volume is that a longer introduction by Burgin, in which he analyzes the nature of these interviews, or the inclusion of Ted Lyon's article on the Borges interview as a critical genre, would have been useful. However, there is a detailed analytical index that is invaluable for seeing the treatment in the interviews of particular themes.

Since Borges has virtually become a part of the English-language literary canon, there is much information here of use to those who may view Borges only as an "international" figure and who have little interest in or regard for his connections with Latin America and, particularly, with Argentina. Since there is a balance between interviews that focus on the purely literary aspects of his work and those (especially by Latin Americanists) that wish to place Borges in a cultural and historical context, Burgin provides an excellent and informative balance of material. [David William Foster]

Steven G. Kellman and Irving Malin, eds. *Into the Tunnel: Readings of Gass's Novel*. Univ. of Delaware Press, 1998. 172 pp. $35.00.

Into the Tunnel makes no attempt to be the ultimate word on William Gass's novel *The Tunnel*. Rather, the goal of editors is to initiate discussion about one of the most baroque and philosophical novels of the century.

There are no Cliff-Notesque outlines or dense, ism-oriented critique in this freewheeling collection (only half the pieces are footnoted). Indeed, James McCourt persuasively ends his argument by simply quoting a passage and asking, "Is there a writer now alive who could top that?" The essays are reactions by very good readers who independently take up with varying degrees of rigor and humor what they find of interest in the novel. Like conversations at a smart party, twelve essays and an interview with Gass circulate around their and their guest-of-honor's concerns: themes of hate as a home-grown product; history as a narrative that creates events; *The Tunnel*'s critical reception; the identification of a loathsome narrator with its author; Gass's formal pyrotechnics, and others. Accordingly there is some overlap as well as contradiction: lively discussion that echoes the seriousness and fun of Gass's "crime and pun," as one contributor puts it.

Among the collection's highlights, Donald J. Greiner articulates well the novel's overarching themes as part of his discussion of its historicism. Rebecca Goldstein takes up the morality of its aesthetics. Arthur Saltzman also compellingly limns Gass's philosophy in his plotless novel which draws readers through its 400,000 words by force of eloquence. Paul Maliszewski, in the collection's major piece, examines Gass's focus on language as the basis for his characterization, plotless construction, and importance; as it unfolds, the essay itself becomes a philosophical act, a critique of naive realism. [Steve Tomasula]

J. P. Donleavy. *Wrong Information Is Being Given out at Princeton*. St. Martin's, 1998. 352 pp. $24.95.

J. P. Donleavy is the author of *The Ginger Man*, one of the century's great comic novels. His latest work, which will hardly be counted among his best, is set in post-World War II New York and traces the adventures of a hapless young composer with an Irish-American background as he tries to make his way among the rich and powerful of the city. Alfonso Stephen O'Kelly'O has the misfortune to be married into a rich family, the Triumphingtons. In this novel the rich are indeed different in how they think and act. Also, they are generally stingy with their money; O'Kelly'O, perpetually short on cash, often must pay the cab fares and restaurant and bar tabs for his wealthy family members. This novel is rich in comical literary and historical allusions: Sylvia's search for her mother echoes and parodies Stephen's search for his father in *Ulysses,* and echoes of *The Great Gatsby* are to be found throughout. The O'Kelly'O family business—bars and liquor stores—is probably modeled on the Kennedys' involvement in similar businesses. Although the narrative doesn't always succeed in this novel due to Donleavy's attempt to include too many minor characters and too many twists to the plot, the examination of O'Kelly'O and the movement toward his moral and artistic victory at the novel's end are most impressive. He is the poor but gifted Irish-American underdog who triumphs over the corrupt WASP ascendancy. However, Donleavy's greatest achievement in this novel is his ability to describe, in such fulsome and elegant detail, post-1945 New York City. Here is a vibrant city energized by the end of the war and populated by citizens, at one level, seeking pleasure wherever they can and, on another level, trying desperately to survive. [Eamonn Wall]

Fernando Pessoa. *The Book of Disquiet.* Trans. Alfred Mac Adam. Exact Change, 1998. 276 pp. $15.95.

This is a reprint of Alfred Mac Adam's superb English-language rendition of the major prose work by the Portuguese modernist Fernando Pessoa (1888-1935). Discovered posthumously in a chaotic trunk in the author's apartment in Lisbon, *Livro do Desassossego* was first published in Portugal in 1982. It is now one of the undisputed classics of twentieth-century literature.

Bilingual in English and Portuguese and powerfully addicted to feelings of nostalgia, estrangement, and exile, Pessoa stands beside Conrad, Nabokov, and Beckett as a writer who used his position as an imaginative outsider to reinvent literary form. Pessoa's particular contribution is to explore new levels of self-consciousness by facing and indeed cultivating "the ill-being that comes from feeling the futility of life." He is a connoisseur of ennui in all its permutations. His narrator, Bernardo Soares, attributes twentieth-century disquietudes to the loss of faith, not just in religion, but in the hopeful doctrines that replaced it, including social equality, aestheticism, science, and philosophy: "We lost all that; we were born orphans of all those consolations."

Infinite longing and finite answers—these are Pessoa's parameters. He contemplates a secular universe with mystical intensity, and achieves a wholly modern, revitalized sense of the self as endlessly elusive and yearning. He recoils, with Beckett, from closure and plot, and subjects himself to a fearful austerity, embodied in the very form of his deliberately openended book of fragments.

Like Pessoa's radically innovative multipersonal poetry, this uniquely ambitious novel makes an essential and illuminating contribution to twentieth-century tradition. It sheds a particular light on modernist, decadent, and absurdist literature. As Mac Adam rightly contends in his introduction, "*The Book of Disquiet* is a literary phenomenon of such magnitude that it must be known." [Philip Landon]

Victor Pelevin. *A Werewolf Problem in Central Russia and Other Stories.* Trans. Andrew Bromfield. New Directions, 1998. 213 pp. $23.95.

Victor Pelevin's new collection offers startling pleasures in its imaginative freedom. Scathingly comic, his vision solicits attention through both insinuation and bravado.

In the title story Pelevin portrays the emotional rush of a young werewolf's awakening to his "cross-over" capabilities. "Vera Pavlovna's Ninth Dream," with roots in Cherneshevsky as well as the worker's state, delivers the main character into an intellectual cul-de-sac reminiscent of Twain's *The Mysterious Stranger.* As the protagonist of "Sleep" attempts to rouse the woozy masses from their comforting primal stupor, Pelevin's satire broadens to include the whole world. His caustic send-ups of latter-day Russian life and mores leave few holds barred.

"Tai Shou Chuan" finds Ch'an the Seventh's uncanny climb up several bureaucratic rungs interrupted by a leading question, dashing his dream of power. Both Pyotr Petrovich's "Tarzan Swing" and a philosophical prison rat's "Ontology of Childhood" mingle detached self-absorption with naive wonder while mapping the compelling topographies of their respective mind-forged manacles. "Bulldozer Driver's Day" proves an occasion for displaying Perestroika's ground zero, where getting soused is the principal preoccupation, a beating the reward for meritorious service. Last, "The Prince of Gosplan" pilots a human Pac-Man through an interlocking set of computer games. Sasha's hack work has him facing perils familiar to devotees of Myst and Doom. Politic, ingenious, and deliberate, he retains a saving grace. Should he make a wrong move, a few keystrokes permit the resumption of his feckless sallies to higher levels.

Each story poses a new problem of perception, the key to which unlocks an unerring internal logic. Pelevin's reach in these stories is considerable, his grasp archly amusing. His penchant for the wild and free should appeal to those for whom contemporary political and social realities contend with whimsical fantasy for outrageous excess. [Michael Pinker]

Jeanette Winterson. *The World and Other Places.* Knopf, 1999. 220 pp. $22.00.

Fans of Jeanette Winterson's laconic prose will find much to enjoy in this, the author's first collection of short fiction. Culling stories from the last twelve years, this book shows that Winterson can sculpt her sentences as precisely in the short form as she does in the novel. Her gift for imagery is startling, whether noticing an aged woman ("with a face like a love-note somebody crushed in his fist") or a dinner table suspended in the air by chains: "an armoury of knives and forks laid out in case the eaters knocked one into the abyss." Despite the deft, self-deprecating irony that finds expression in her characters, Winterson's lyricism is the central note struck throughout, as in this passage from "Adventure of a Lifetime": "I started to think about Hansel and Gretel and how they found their way through the forest by leaving a trail of stones. We left nothing behind but the heat from our bodies and that soon chilled."

One of the most delightful things about this book is its range; Winterson proves herself equally adept at personal narrative ("The 24-Hour Dog"), fable ("The Three Friends"), speculative fiction ("Disappearance I") and arty metatext ("The Poetics of Sex"). Her story "Newton" (which contains the all-time great sentence: "There's no room for the dead unless you treat them as ornamental") lengthens this reach even farther. As in her novels, Winterson is able to enunciate a feminist politics without leadening her prose, and her facility for portraying strong women (such as the Artemis who quietly kills a brutish Orion in a reimagined mythology) is balanced here by complex male characters (see "Atlantic Crossing," "The Green Man," or the title story). "Using my compass I write to you," Winterson says in her afterword, and indeed, she directs these stories to her readers with unerring aim. [Eric Lorberer]

Silvio Gaggi. *From Text to Hypertext: Decentering the Subject in Fiction, Film, the Visual Arts and Electronic Media.* Univ. of Pennsylvania Press, 1998. 169 pp. Paper: $14.95.

A shift in representation of the self is the topic of Silvio Gaggi's lucid *From Text to Hypertext.* Specifically, Gaggi examines static images, printed literary texts, films, and hypertexts to demonstrate that in many art and literary works, the Cartesian self has been replaced by a much more contingent, less self-directed, less central entity: the human subject.

His baseline is Jan van Eyck's *The Wedding of Arnolfini,* a fifteenth-century painting that valorizes the self through a language of perspective, gesture, and other signs. Against this witness Gaggi contrasts the shattered viewpoints of Picasso's cubist work and Cindy Sherman's "movie stills," self-portraits in which Sherman takes on, in chameleon fashion, the various female personae of B-movie stereotypes. The chapter on literature outlines the subject as a product of discourse by reading Joseph Conrad's *Heart of Darkness,* William Faulkner's *As I Lay Dying,* and Italo Calvino's *If on a winter's night a traveler.* Calvino's work especially makes Gaggi's case in its subversion of textual authority. By contrast, less pointed examples, e.g., the modernist works, or as in the chapter on film, fairly conventional commercial movies, seem less useful. Still, as in Gaggi's discussion of hypertext, the attention to form and how various stances toward subjectivity are embedded in form provide a refreshing approach to the ontological implications of aesthetics. His analysis of spatial quality (be it the space of perspective, camera movement, or eye movement through a text) is situated within the wider world and informed most by Baudrillard, Jameson, and Lacan (especially Lacan's mirror phase). Gaggi leads readers through all of this with a thoughtful clarity and ends his argument with the balance of a humanist, searching for a way to reconcile the deconstruction of the self with those who ask: "On behalf of what should we reject totalitarianism?" [Steve Tomasula]

Maxim D. Shrayer. *The World of Nabokov's Short Stories.* Univ. of Texas Press, 1999. 432 pp. $49.95.

Shrayer's book is a brilliant reading of Nabokov's stories. He tries to stress the "otherworld"—the world which is far removed from conventional constructions of the afterlife. He makes a wonderful case for the fact that Nabokov's stories, especially the ones written in Russian, are an attempt to force the reader to see the "markers" of the otherworld in the "small Alpine" (Nabokov's phrase) form.

Thus he reads these "open-ended" stories in a detailed way. He demonstrates shrewdly that the Russian stories embody hints of the otherworld. Consider his lengthy, absorbing study of "The Return of Chorb" (written in 1925): "Chorb is obsessed with a maniacal quest of his dead wife's perfect image." Chorb is, as Shrayer writes, an Orpheus attempting to find his Eurydice. The story has its origin in Ovid's *Metamorphoses*—and it points to the fact that Nabokov constantly tries to recover the past, to make it present. (Here is the entrance of memory as a preoccupation.) Shrayer muses about the deceptive linguistic plays with Chorb's name; he informs us that the "markedness" of otherness is found in the metrical effects in the last three lines.

I have not done justice to Shrayer's exciting criticism. His first book already demonstrates his erudition—his ability to trace patterns which I had never thought of. I admire Shrayer—and I envy his rare talent. [Irving Malin]

Perry Anderson. *The Origins of Postmodernity.* Verso, 1998. 143 pp. Paper: $16.00; Fredric Jameson. *The Cultural Turn: Selected Writings on the Postmodern, 1983-1998.* Verso, 1998. 206 pp. Paper: $16.00.

These two books are meant to be companion pieces, but each one in itself provides an invaluable background picture of the so-called postmodern world lying behind the literary, artistic, and other cultural expressions of recent times. Initially planned as an introduction to Jameson's collection, Anderson's genealogy of intellectual origins offers a series of succinct and energizing characterizations of attempts to define postmodernity. His range is international and covers various thinkers from the last six decades, from Federico de Onìs, Arnold Toynbee, and Charles Olson up through Ihab Hassan, Jean-François Lyotard, Jürgen Habermas, and Jameson himself, who emerges as the hero of this book. Nevertheless, Anderson's overview of Jameson's career contains several productive criticisms, chief of which is his charge that Jameson overemphasizes the role of economics and downplays that of politics in his theoretical program.

Literary-critical discussions of postmodernism tend to be tedious and trivial, but the multidisciplinary assessments by Anderson and Jameson are quite the opposite. Anderson's two purposes are to trace the key changes in the idea of postmodernity and, less extensively, to speculate on the structural and geopolitical conditions that have produced both the idea and the changes. Jameson's essays pursue this second endeavor more thoroughly, and they document numerous significant and startling links between postmodern cultural expressions and structural developments in global politics, society, and above all, economics. In its entirety, Jameson's corpus on postmodernity attempts, by considering literature and other cultural expressions as "socially symbolic acts," to present a totalizing historical reconstruction of the last few years of world history. Judging by the insightful and sometimes even mind-blowing essays in *The Cultural Turn,* Anderson may well be right in claiming that it offers the most satisfactory theoretical reconstruction to date. [Thomas Hove]

Nina Berberova. *The Ladies from St. Petersburg: Three Novellas.* Trans. Marian Schwartz. New Directions, 1998. 122 pp. $19.95.

Nina Berberova possessed a rare talent. The last writer of the post-czarist creative exodus to be discovered by the English-speaking world, the friend of Khodasevich and biographer of Blok, she wrote brilliantly. Unknown outside exile circles for most of her life, at last Berberova's artistry begs its due. This new collection, two early stories and perhaps her last one, ably translated, should appeal to readers for their deft craftsmanship and subtle formal elegance.

The title story follows a threadbare aristocratic mother and child on holiday to the Russian hinterland on the eve of the Revolution. When Varvara Ivanovna suddenly dies, leaving her eligible Margarita alone among strangers, funeral preparations reveal the peasants' contempt for their betters near to boiling, as if in anticipation of what will soon strike home. Yet Margarita's distressed concern for her mother's proper burial almost seems to belong to another world; an era is over. Likewise, self-absorbed Zoya Andreyevna, fleeing Petrograd after 1917, seeks little but a semblance of shelter and stability in her newly diminished situation. Still, the pursuing Reds prove far less threatening than those among whom she would reside, resentful harpies whose jealousy of aristocratic pretentions finds a proper target in Zoya's effete helplessness. Finally, "The Big City" renders a new émigré's fantastic chase after self-discovery through a metropolis modeled on New York, replete with kaleidoscopic urbanities out of Fritz Lang or Terry Gilliam's *Brazil.* As the unnamed protagonist reflects after stumbling through his personal maze, "I realized then that every person brings whatever he can to this big city"—not least, his sense of America.

Berberova's style resurrects an aristocracy of outlook and taste reminiscent of Nabokov, of a Russia beyond socialism. After sampling these delightful stories, one looks forward to further sojourns into the labyrinth of her art. [Michael Pinker]

Lawrence Rainey. *Institutions of Modernism: Literary Elites & Public Culture.* Yale Univ. Press, 1999. 240 pp. $25.00.

This is the second book within the last two years I have read that attempts to explain modernism ("high modernism," that is) via money/investment/ patrons. Rainey's book is smarter and more precise than *Who Paid for Modernism?,* but it is also more subversive for its smartness and precision. Unlike the former, this book holds back its accusations until the evidence has been gathered, and then the hammer falls on the motives of Pound, Joyce, Eliot, H. D., et al. I don't want to inspect the rightness or wrongness of what Rainey argues but rather guess at where all of this is leading. Both books' subtext is that modernism purposely cut itself off from the "public," and both say that it did so as a kind of marketing tool: if you can't interest a million readers in your book and thereby become wealthy, then go after ten people with money who both appreciate the work and also see it as a solid investment. The modernists are at long last exposed! It's all about money! They and their patrons were in pursuit of money—the same motives as the popular artist—but the patrons were willing to wait a generation for the payoff, and besides they got to go to better parties and mix with the right people. Underlying all of this is a populist axe to grind: that the People get left out, the Public is bewildered and prevented from entering the discourse, and the Common Man (who was it who said that the thing about the Common Man is that he is *common?*) had no access to this art. So something is afoot here and one should always be wary when "the public" is used to argue almost anything. I do not know whether these books (and no doubt articles and books to come) have an agenda of putting the last nail in modernism's coffin or are somehow a response to the theory-based exclusivity now present in academia (e.g., "Anything and everything is a fucking text but only *we* are privileged to be able to decode it") or, at least in the United States, a resurgence on the part of government to make art synonymous with mass consumption or perhaps commercial publishing's way of authenticating best-sellers and why the public (incidentally urged on by publishers' enormous marketing budgets to position their books before Oprah's eyes) should decide what art is.

In his introduction Rainey anticipates the criticism that the works themselves are not discussed and responds with: "I reject the idea that history or theory are acceptable only if they take on the role of humble handmaiden to the aesthetic artifact." In other words art is out there to fend for itself: fine. But Rainey's book and its argument are in themselves establishing a handmaiden relationship, one in which writers' nasty economic motives are inspected and the work itself made irrelevant (of course, of course). I suppose the subject of whether patrons allowed for the development of a certain kind of art (namely, that Pound was able to do what he wanted rather than having to worry about a popular audience) is passingly interesting, but then so are any number of other subjects that bear on these issues: agents; friends who help friends get published; the advantage of being published by a large commercial house; universities employing writers, and on and on. Each of these factors has some bearing on the production, accessibility, popularity, and "importance" of writers, books, and movements, but ultimately have little or nothing to do with *quality* (a naughty word, I know) of what results. I would rather use a lotto method for determining such things than to depend upon the *public,* though I would prefer the public to, for instance, the *New York Times Book Review.* [John O'Brien]

Books Received

Adams, Hazard. *Many Pretty Toys*. State Univ. of New York Press, 1999. No price given. (F)

Allouache, Merzak. *Bab el-Oued*. Trans. Angela M. Brewer. Lynne Rienner, 1998. Paper: $13.95. (F)

Amburn, Ellis. *Subterranean Kerouac*. St. Martin's, 1998. $27.95. (NF)

Anastas, Benjamin. *An Underachiever's Diary*. Spike, 1999. Paper: $10.00. (F)

Andersen, Hans Christian. *Travels*. Trans. and ed. by Anastazia Little. Green Integer, 1999. Paper: $12.95. (F)

Argueta, Manlio. *Little Red Riding Hood in the Red Light District*. Trans. Edward Waters Hood. Curbstone, 1998. Paper: $14.95. (F)

Arnold, Edwin T., and Dianne C. Luce. *Perspectives on Cormac McCarthy*. Univ. Press of Mississippi, 1999. Paper: $18.00. (NF)

Avery, Valeen Tippetts. *From Mission to Madness: Last Son of the Mormon Prophet*. Univ. of Illinois Press, 1998. Paper: $19.95. (NF)

Ball, Gordon. *'66 Frames*. Coffee House, 1999. Paper: $15.95. (NF)

Ballard, J. G. *The Day of Creation*. Farrar, Straus & Giroux, 1999. Paper: $13.00. (F)

Ballard, J. G. *War Fever*. Farrar, Straus & Giroux, 1999. Paper: $10.00. (F)

Bank, Melissa. *The Girls' Guide to Hunting and Fishing*. Viking, 1999. $23.95. (F)

Banner, Keith. *The Life I Lead*. Knopf, 1999. $23.00. (F)

Barnes, Julian. *England, England*. Knopf, 1999. $23.00. (F)

Bataille, Georges. *The Collected Poems of Georges Bataille*. Trans. and intro. Mark Spitzer. Dufour, 1999. Paper: $15.95. (F)

Beard, Richard. *X20: A Novel of (Not) Smoking*. Spike, 1999. Paper: $12.00. (F)

Beard, Richard. *Damascus*. Arcade, 1999. $23.95. (F)

Berberova, Nina. *The Book of Happiness*. New Directions, 1999. $23.95. (F)

Berressem, Hanjo. *Lines of Desire: Reading Gombrowicz's Fiction with Lacan*. Northwestern Univ. Press, 1998. $79.95. (NF)

Breznik, Melitta. *Night Duty*. Steerforth, 1999. Paper: $12.00. (F)

Bigelow, Gary. *Sisters of Interment*. Red Crane, 1998. Paper: $16.95. (F)

Birkerts, Sven. *Readings*. Graywolf, 1999. Paper: $16.00. (NF)

Blanchot, Maurice. *The Station Hill Blanchot Reader*. Ed. George Quasha. Trans. Lydia Davis, Paul Auster, and Robert Lamberton. Station Hill, 1999. Paper: $29.95. (F & NF)

Blatnik, Andrej. *Skinswaps*. Trans. Tamara Soban. Northwestern Univ. Press, 1998. Paper: $14.95. (F)

Bloch, Ernst. *Literary Essays*. Trans. Andrew Joron, et al. Stanford Univ. Press, 1998. No price given. (NF)

Bolger, Dermot, ed. *Finbar's Hotel*. Harvest, 1999. Paper: $13.00. (F)

Borges, Jorge Luis. *Everything and Nothing*. New Directions, 1999. Paper:

$7.50. (F)

Breckenridge, Donald. *Rockaway Wherein*. Red Dust, 1998. Paper: $6.95. (F)

Buechner, Frederick. *The Storm*. Harper San Francisco, 1998. $18.00. (F)

Canetti, Elias. *The Memoirs of Elias Canetti*. Farrar Straus & Giroux, 1999. $40.00. (NF)

Cather, Willa. *Obscure Destinies*. Historical essay and explanatory notes by Kari A. Ronning, textual essay by Frederick M. Link with Kari A. Ronning and Mark Kamrath. Univ. of Nebraska Press, 1998. $65.00. (F)

Chabon, Michael. *Werewolves in Their Youth*. Random House, 1999. $22.95. (F)

Chaplin, Gordon. *Dark Wind: A Survivor's Tale of Love and Loss*. Atlantic, 1999. $22.00. (NF)

Chaudhuri, Amit. *Freedom Song*. Knopf, 1999. $24.00. (F)

Chenoweth, Avery. *Wingtips*. Johns Hopkins Univ. Press, 1999. $22.50. (F)

Chimo. *Lila Says*. Scribner, 1999. $20.00. (F)

Ch'ing-wen, Cheng. *Three-Legged Horse*. Ed. Pang-yaun Chi. Columbia Univ. Press, 1999. $22.95. (F)

Chute, Carolyn. *Snow Man*. Harcourt Brace, 1999. $23.00. (F)

Condé, Mary, and Thorunn Lonsdale. *Caribbean Women Writers: Fiction in English*. St. Martin's, 1999. Paper: $17.95. (NF)

Cook, Méira. *The Blood Girls*. Overlook, 1999. $22.95. (F)

Cortázar, Julio. *Cronopios and Famas*. New Directions, 1999. Paper: $12.95. (F)

Coundouriotis, Eleni. *Claiming History: Colonialism, Ethnography, and the Novel*. Columbia Univ. Press, 1999. Paper: $16.50. (NF)

Crawford, Lynn. *Blow*. Hard Press, 1998. No price given. (F)

Cribb, T. J., ed. *Imagined Commonwealths: Cambridge Essays on Commonwealth and International Literature in English*. St. Martin's, 1999. $55.00. (NF)

Crockett, Roger A. *Understanding Friedrich Dürrenmatt*. Univ. of South Carolina Press, 1998. $29.95. (NF)

Dali, Salvador. *Oui: The Paranoid-Critical Revolution: Writings 1927-1933*. Exact Change, 1999. Paper: $13.95. (NF)

Darper, Robert. *Hadrian's Walls*. Knopf, 1999. $23.00. (F)

de la Baume, Cécile. *Crush*. Trans. Ramona Desfleurs. Grove, 1999. Paper: $11.00. (F)

de Mandiargues, André Pieyre. *Portrait of an Englishman in His Chateau*. Dedalus, 1999. Paper: $12.99. (F)

DiBlasi, Debra. *Prayers of an Accidental Nature*. Coffee House, 1999. Paper: $13.95. (F)

Dillard, Annie. *For the Time Being*. Knopf, 1999. $22.00. (NF)

Dixon, Stephen. *Sleep*. Coffee House, 1999. Paper: $15.95. (F)

Donaldson, George, and Mara Kalnins, *D. H. Lawrence in Italy and England*. St. Martin's Press, 1999. $55.00. (NF)

[Doolittle, Hilda] H.D., *The Gift*. Ed. Jane Augustine. Univ. of Florida Press, 1998. $49.95. (NF)

Ellis, Bret Easton. *Glamorama*. Knopf, 1999. $25.00. (F)

Englander, Nathan. *For the Relief of Unbearable Urges*. Knopf, 1999. $23.00. (F)

Farrell, Kirby. *Post-Traumatic Culture: Injury and Interpretation in the Nineties*. Johns Hopkins Univ. Press, 1998. Paper: $17.95. (NF)

Feuerwerker, Yi-tsi Mei. *Ideology, Power, Text: Self-Representation and the Peasant "Other" in Modern Chinese Literature.* Stanford Univ. Press, 1998. $49.50. (NF)

Fitch, Janet. *White Oleander.* Little, Brown, 1999. $24.00. (F)

Galligan, Edward L. *The Truth of Uncertainty: Beyond Ideology in Science and Literature.* Univ. of Missouri Press, 1998. $29.95. (NF)

Golden, Jeff. *Forest Blood.* Wellstone, 1999. Paper: $15.00. (F)

Goonetillerke, D. C. R. A. *Salman Rushdie.* St. Martin's, 1998. $35.00. (NF)

Gunderson, Joanna. *The Field.* Red Dust, 1998. Paper: $10.95. (F)

Gunn, Kirsty. *This Place You Return to Is Home.* Atlantic, 1999. $22.00. (F)

Guterson, David. *East of the Mountains.* Harcourt Brace, 1999. $25.00. (F)

Hallwas, John E. *The Bootlegger: A Story of Small-Town America.* Univ. of Illinois Press, 1998. $24.95. (NF)

Harris, Mark. *Speed.* Univ. of Nebraska Press, 1998. Paper: $15.00. (F)

Hicks, Michael. *Sixties Rock: Garage, Psychedelic, and Other Satisfactions.* Univ. of Illinois Press, 1999. $26.95. (NF)

Hinojosa, Francisco. *Hectic Ethics.* Trans. Kurt Hollander. City Lights, 1998. Paper: $9.95. (F)

Hollingshead, Greg. *The Healer.* Harper Flamingo, 1999. $24.00. (F)

Hotschnig, Alois. *Leonardo's Hands.* Univ. of Nebraska Press, 1999. Paper: $12.00. (F)

Irwin, Robert. *Prayer-Cushions of the Flesh.* Dedalus, 1999. Paper: $11.99. (F)

Jaffe, Harold. *Sex for the Millennium.* FC2, 1999. Paper: $9.00. (F)

Jen, Gish. *Who's Irish?* Knopf, 1999. $22.00 (F)

Jennings, Kate. *Snake.* Back Bay, 1999. Paper: $12.00. (F)

Jenny, Zoë. *The Pollen Room.* Trans. Elizabeth Gaffney. Simon & Schuster, 1999. $20.00. (F)

Ji-moon, Suh, ed. *The Golden Phoenix: Seven Contemporary Korean Short Stories.* Lynne Rienner, 1998. Paper: $19.95. (F)

Kacirk, Jeffrey. *Forgotten English.* Morrow, 1997. Paper: $11.00. (NF)

Kanafani, Ghassan. *Men in the Sun and Other Palestinian Stories.* Lynne Rienner, 1998. Paper: $11.50. (F)

Kashner, Sam. *Sinatraland.* Overlook, 1999. $22.95. (F)

Kates, Erica, ed. *On the Couch: Great American Stories about Therapy.* Atlantic, 1999. Paper: $14.00. (F)

Kaye, John. *Stars Screaming.* Atlantic, 1999. Paper: $13.00. (F)

Kreilkamp, Vera. *The Anglo-Irish Novel and the Big House.* Syracuse Univ. Press, 1998. No price given. (NF)

MacGowan, Christopher, ed. *The Letters of Denise Levertov and William Carlos Williams.* New Directions, 1998. $24.95. (NF)

MacMillan, Ian. *Village of a Million Spirits: A Novel of the Treblinka Uprising.* Steerforth, 1999. $24.00. (F)

Mahony, Christina Hunt. *Contemporary Irish Literature.* St. Martin's, 1999. Paper: $18.95. (NF)

Mamet, David. *The Chinaman: Poems.* Overlook, 1999. $19.95. (P)

Martin, Valerie. *Italian Fever.* Knopf, 1999. $22.00. (F)

McCabe, Patrick. *Breakfast on Pluto.* Harper Flamingo, 1998. $22.00. (F)

McDermott, Alice. *Charming Billy.* Dell, 1998. Paper: $12.95. (F)

Miller, Anita. *Uncollecting Cheever.* Rowman & Littlefield, 1998. $27.95. (NF)

Mnookin, Wendy. *To Get Here*. BOA Editions, 1999. Paper: $12.50. (F)

Mojtabai, A.G. *Soon*. Zoland, 1998. $22.00. (F)

Mueller, Marnie. *The Climate of the Country*. Curbstone, 1999. $24.95. (F)

Mutawa, Vusamazulu Credo. *Indaba My Children: African Folktales*. Grove, 1999. Paper: $16.00. ((F)

Nabokov, Vladimir. *Speak, Memory*. Intro. Brian Boyd. Knopf, 1999. $17.00. (NF)

Naslund, Sena Jeter. *The Disobedience of Water*. David R. Godine, 1999. $21.95. (F)

Neilson, Jim. *Warring Fictions: Cultural Politics and the Vietnam War Narrative*. Univ. Press of Mississippi, 1998. Paper: $18.00. (NF)

Offill, Jenny. *Last Things*. Farrar, Straus & Giroux, 1999. $23.00. (F)

Paley, Vivian Gussin. *The Kindness of Children*. Harvard Univ. Press, 1999. $18.95. (NF)

Patchen, Kenneth. *The Memoirs of a Shy Pornographer*. New Directions, 1999. Paper: $14.00. (F)

Pérez-Reverte, Arturo. *The Fencing Master*. Harcourt Brace, 1999. $24.00. (F)

Pessoa, Fernando. *The Book of Disquiet: Composed by Bernardo Soares, Assistant Bookkeeper in the City of Lisbon*. Trans. Alfred Mac Adam. Exact Change, 1998. Paper: $15.95. (F)

Plante, David. *The Age of Terror*. St. Martin's, 1999. $24.95. (F)

Polansky, Steven. *Nine Stories*. Ohio State Univ. Press, 1999. Paper: $15.95. (F)

Pomerance, Murray. *Magia D'Amore*. Sun & Moon, 1999. Paper: $12.95. (F)

Romalis, Shelly. *Pistol Packin' Mama: Aunt Molly Jackson and the Politics of Folksong*. Univ. of Illinois Press, 1999. Paper: $18.95. (NF)

Rosset, Barney. *Evergreen Review Reader 1967-1973*. Four Walls Eight Windows, 1999. Paper: $24.95. (NF)

Rubinsky, Holley, ed. *The Journey Prize Anthology*. McClelland & Stewart, 1999. Paper: $15.95. (F)

Sawyer-Lauçanno, Christopher. *An Invisible Spectator*. Grove, 1999. Paper: $15.00. (NF)

Schlueter, Paul, and Jane Schlueter. *Encyclopedia of British Women Writers*. Rutgers Univ. Press, 1999. $60.00. Paper: $28.00. (NF)

Shaked, Gershon, ed. *Six Israeli Novellas*. David R. Godine, 1999. $27.95. (F)

Shepard, Lucius. *Barnacle Bill the Spacer and Other Stories*. Four Walls Eight Windows, 1999. Paper: $14.95. (F)

Shwartz, Ronald B. *For the Love of Books*. Grosset/Putnam, 1999. $24.95. (F)

Solotaroff, Ted. *Truth Comes in Blows*. Norton, 1998. $33.95. (NF)

Solzhenitsyn, Aleksander. *November 1916: The Red Wheel II*. Farrar, Straus & Giroux, 1999. $35.00. (F)

Thompson, Jean. *Who Do You Love*. Harcourt Brace, 1999. $23.00. (F)

Trow, George W. S. *My Pilgrim's Progress*. Pantheon, 1999. $24.00. (NF)

Tryzna, Tomek. *Girl Nobody*. Fourth Estate, 1999. £10.99. (F)

Waddington, James. *Bad to the Bone*. Dedalus, 1999. Paper: $12.99. (F)

Webb, Don. *The Double*. St. Martin's, 1998. $22.95. (F)

White, Edmund. *Marcel Proust*. Penguin, 1999. $19.95. (NF)

Winslow, Don. *California Fire and Life*. Knopf, 1999. $23.00. (F)

Wolitzer, Meg. *Surrender, Dorothy*. Scribner, 1999. $22.00. (F)

Yamanaka, Lois-Ann. *Heads by Harry*. Farrar, Straus & Giroux, 1999.

$24.00. (F)
Yatromanolakis, Yoryis. *Eroticon*. Dedalus, 1999. Paper: $13.99. (F)
Zinovieva-Annibal, Lydia. *The Tragic Menagerie*. Trans. and Intro. Jane
Costlow. Northwestern Univ. Press, 1999. Paper: $16.95. (F)
Zweig, Martha. *Vinegar Bone*. Wesleyan Univ. Press, 1999. Paper: $11.95. (F)

Studies in 20th Century Literature

A journal devoted to literary theory and practical criticism

Volume 23, No. 2 (Summer, 1999)

Special Issue in preparation:

Russian Culture of the 1990s
Guest Editor: Helena Goscilo

Silvia Sauter, Editor
Kansas State University
Eisenhower 104
Manhattan, KS 66506-1003
Submissions in:
Russian and Spanish

Jordan Stump, Editor
University of Nebraska
PO Box 880318
Lincoln, NE 68588-0318
Submissions in:
French and German

Subscriptions

Institutions—$30 for one year ($55 for two years)
Individuals—$25 for one year ($45 for two years)
Single issues—$15.00 (add $8 for Air Mail)

CHICAGO REVIEW

| A JOURNAL OF WRITING & CRITICAL EXCHANGE |

IN RECENT ISSUES
Susan Howe
Tom Pickard
John Koethe
Ciaran Carson
Greg Miller
Jody Gladding
Ronald Johnson

SPECIAL FEATURES
Basil Bunting
Peter Dale Scott
Robert Duncan

Subscribe now and receive our recent issue on contemporary poetry & poetics. Free upon request.

SUBSCRIPTIONS **$18**
SAMPLE COPIES **$6**

UNIVERSITY OF CHICAGO
5801 SOUTH KENWOOD AVE • CHICAGO IL **60637**
chicago-review@uchicago.edu

college Literature

Kostas Myrsiades, Editor

CL is published in Winter, Spring, and Fall.
Regular rates, USA: institutions $48 per year; individuals $24 per year. Other countries add $10.

A triannual journal of scholarly criticism serving the needs of college/university teachers by providing access to innovative ways of studying and teaching new bodies of literature and experiencing old literatures in new ways.

The journal provides usable, readable, and timely material designed to keep its readers abreast of new developments and shifts in the theory and practice of literature by covering the full range of what is presently being read and taught as well as what should be read and taught in the college literature classroom.

CL accepts papers that deal with textual analysis, literary theory, and pedagogy for today's changing college classrooms. Manuscripts should between 8000 to 10000 words.

Address all correspondence to

COLLEGE LITERATURE
210 E. Rosedale Avenue
West Chester University
West Chester, PA 19383
610-436-2901/2275
Fax 610-436-3212
collit@wcupa.edu

Forthcoming issues

Cultural Violence
Teaching Literature at the End of the Millennium
Beat Poets
Medieval Culture
Literature and Art
Working Class Literature

and a General issue every Spring

Prairie Schooner
has a long tradition of
publishing the best
contemporary writing
available.
As *Literary Magazine
Review* says, "Prairie
Schooner rolls along,
avoiding the quagmires
of fads and schisms,
steadfastly defining the
American idiom."

We're old but
we're not stuffy.

George Garrett

George Garrett
The Elizabethan Trilogy

Edited by Brooke Horvath and Irving Malin
Introduction by Fred Chappell

This new volume is a collection of essays and poems on George Garrett's best-selling trilogy of Elizabethan England: *Death of the Fox*, *The Succession*, and *Entered from the Sun*.

Contributors of the essays include Richard Betts, "'To Dream of Kings': George Garrett's *The Succession*"; Nicholas Delbanco, "*The Succession*: A Novel of Elizabeth and James"; Joseph Dewey, "'A Golden Age for Fantasticks': Imagination, Faith, and Mistery in *Entered from the Sun*"; R. H. W. Dillard, "The Elizabethan Novels: *Death of the Fox* and *The Succession*"; Thomas Fleming, "'The Historical Consciousness of George Garrett"; Reginald Gibbons, "George Garrett's Whole New World: *The Succession*"; Steven G. Kellman, "Who Killed Kit Marlowe? Who Wants to Know?"'; Irving Malin, "Hermetic Fox-Hunting"; Joseph W. Reed, "Settling Marlowe's Hash"; W. R. Robinson, "Imagining the Individual: George Garrett's *Death of the Fox*"; David R. Slavitt, "A Twentieth Century *Fox*—in the Warner Brothers' Chicken Coop"; Monroe K. Spears

"A Trilogy Complete, A Past Recaptured"; Walter Sullivan, "Time Past and Time Present: Garrett's *Entered from the Sun*"; Richard Tillinghast, "The Fox, Gloriana, Kit Marlowe, and Sundry"; Tom Whalen, "Eavesdropping in the Dark: The Opening(s) of George Garrett's *Entered from the Sun*"; Allen Wier, "The Scars of Flesh and Spirit or How He Pictures It: George Garrett's *Entered from the Sun*."

Brendan Galvin ("Your Messenger of 1566") and Laurence Goldstein ("In Praise of *Entered from the Sun*") contribute poems to the volume.

Fred Chappell notes in the introduction that "the trilogy swarms me over: it is full to bursting with a history that seems to have more complexity than the actual life I am living and it has caused me to interpret in its terms events I witness firsthand and even participate in."

BROOKE HORVATH is a professor of English at Kent State University. IRVING MALIN is a retired English professor living in Forest Hills, New York.

Available from
Texas Review Press
Texas A & M U P Consortium
800-826-8911

George Garrett
1-881515-13-3 cloth $26.00
1-881515-14-1 paper $15.00

6x9. 200 pp.
Literary Criticism.